Having worked in the Civil Aviation for thirty-five years, and recently retired, I have turned to my first love: The Royal Navy in WWII. Having been a keen student of naval history and having had a few award-winning naval modelling articles published, this is my second foray with Captain Alan Lee.

This is a work of fiction. Names, characters, businesses, places, events and incidents are either the product of the author's imagination or used in a fictitious manner. Any resemblance to actual persons, living or dead, or actual events is purely coincidental.

End of the Beginning

Ron Wilkinson

End of the Beginning

Vanguard Press

VANGUARD PAPERBACK

© Copyright 2023
Ron Wilkinson

The right of Ron Wilkinson to be identified as author of this work has been asserted by them in accordance with the Copyright, Designs and Patents Act 1988.

All Rights Reserved

No reproduction, copy or transmission of this publication may be made without written permission.
No paragraph of this publication may be reproduced, copied or transmitted save with the written permission of the publisher, or in accordance with the provisions of the Copyright Act 1956 (as amended).

Any person who commits any unauthorised act in relation to this publication may be liable to criminal prosecution and civil claims for damages.

A CIP catalogue record for this title is available from the British Library.

ISBN 978 1 80016 546 5

*Vanguard Press is an imprint of
Pegasus Elliot Mackenzie Publishers Ltd.*
www.pegasuspublishers.com

First Published in 2023

**Vanguard Press
Sheraton House Castle Park
Cambridge England**

Printed & Bound in Great Britain

To all the friends and family who have supported and encouraged this work. In particular, my long-suffering wife Carol, Steve who has given me many ideas and suggestions, Dave and Lyn, Mark, Mike, J.P. and Janet. And finally, to my dear friend, Alf, who has crossed the bar.

Contents

Introduction 9
Chapter 1 12
Chapter 2 26
Chapter 3 48
Chapter 4 65
Chapter 5 78
Chapter 6 84
Chapter 7 93
Chapter 8 109
Chapter 9 121
Chapter 10 136
Chapter 11 154
Glossary 165

Introduction

HMS Preston, and her captain are fictional. The actions you have read in book one, 'In Our Darkest Hour', and this volume are based on true events. Obviously, Preston was not involved in them, nor was her captain. The 'Town, Southampton, Colony' class light cruisers did exist. They were well-built, fine-looking ships, and the Royal Navy were justifiably proud of them. They served in every ocean in the world with distinction and suffered appalling damage and tragic losses. Of the twenty-one built six were lost, two others so severely damaged they had to be rebuilt, and many others so badly damaged they barely made it home to a safe port. Their design was 'frozen' at an early stage, and it became very apparent that their initial Anti-Aircraft Armament was woefully deficient. (So poor in fact that HMS Gloucester and HMS Fiji were lost because they ran out of ammunition and were firing practice rounds at their aerial tormentors). However, 'H.M Treasury' insisted they were completed as is. From the early 1930's, the Royal Navy had been banking on a Vickers .5in multiple machine gun for its close range A.A. weapon, which even during its development did not have the stopping power the Admiralty was looking for. This was one of the many factors that accounted for the tragic loses of HM ships in the early war years. (Most warships in the Mediterranean, in the time period of this book, had 'acquired' captured Italian and German weapons. The soldiers that were being evacuated, left behind many rifles, Bren and Vickers machine guns, plus tons of ammunition, which was gladly snapped up to supplement the ships close range armament.)

It was only later when the superlative Swiss 20mm Oerlikon, and Swedish 40mm Bofors guns became available, along with Radar, Long Range Aircraft, Code Breaking etc. that things slowly turned in the allies' favour at sea. I must add a personal word here, about the excellent help and support that the USA, and their Naval dockyards gave. As so many seriously damaged R.N. warships, they struggled across the Atlantic to be repaired, refitted as an exceptional gesture of goodwill.

The Captain, and some of the characters, are genuine, but I have changed the names to protect their identity. In my early work years, I spent a lot of time with ex Royal Navy Veterans from WWII. It was fascinating and humbling to hear their experiences, good and bad. I did take notes at the time, and put them away for future use, and living in the real world, they were forgotten about. Unfortunately, these brave men have all 'crossed the bar', and it is my personnel regret that they never got to see this tribute to them. It was much later, when I heard of the loss of one of my dearest friends, I decided I wanted these memories to be heard. While the 'Official' history of the events at sea are available in many formats, I wanted the personal experiences recorded, and woven into this story, so the general public could understand the stress, terror, lack of sleep, these men had to endure. The single lines of text I have added are their stories, are genuine, and they *did* happen.

For all Royal Navy ships, 'That are still on patrol', RIP.

Chapter 1

The ship slowly rolled over on her port side. Captain Alan Lee R.N. scrambled over the rail, and walked down the ship's side, and across the barnacle encrusted lower hull. He stopped momentarily to look around to make sure what was left of his crew had got away, and as tradition dictated, he was the last to leave the ship. Moving as fast as his exhausted body would let him, he doggy paddled towards a partially submerged Carley float. The fuel oil which covered the distance to the float, was particularly thick, which hampered his feeble attempts to swim. Eventually helping hands grabbed him and unceremoniously hauled him aboard. "Come on, mate, we got you! Make way, lads, it's the skipper." Lee collapsed across the side of the raft and retched his guts up in an attempt to clear his lungs of the oil.

A voice shouts, "She's going." Lee raised his head and watched as HIS ship *"Proud Preston"* slowly submerged below the warm Mediterranean Sea. The same voice shouted, "Three cheers for the ship, Hip Hip." That was the time Lee broke down and cried for his lost crew mates.

A shadow fell across the raft, as *HMS Wilton* slowed down to collect the survivors. Many hands helped his crew to climb the scrambling nets onto *Wilton's* iron deck. A seawater hose had been set up to wash down the men as they came aboard, to rid them of the filthy oil. After which their clothes were stripped of them and rough woollen blankets passed around. Standing shivering, in just his underwear, Lee was approached by *Wilton's* young First Lieutenant. "Sir, Captain's complements, would you follow me to the Captain's cabin?"

"Are all my men onboard No. 1?" The noise from the ship's telegraph indicated that *Wilton* was underway, following the remnants of the convoy.

"Yes, sir, we have onboard everybody we could save, sir, it's not many. I am sorry." Lee nodded and followed the Officer to the Captain's cabin. Inside was the steward. "I have run you a bath, sir, and my Captain has left some clothes for you, and when you are ready, I will serve lunch."

A feeble "Thank You" from Lee. Overhead he could hear the alarm rattlers go off, and a stampede of sea boots, as the crew ran to action stations. Lee sank into the warm water and with a block of 'Pusser's soap' began scrubbing at the remaining clinging oil. Overhead he could hear the cacophony of exploding bombs, the deeper boom of the ship's main armament firing and the clatter of empty shell casing landing on the deck above him. But Lee didn't care; it was somebody else's turn to fight the enemy. The steward was kindness itself, recognizing that Lee would only want a light lunch, and strong sweet tea, and a glass of Pusser's Rum, which made Lee retch again, and which brought up a belly full of oil, but made Lee feel a whole lot better. Later, dressed in the *Wilton's* Captain's shirt and trousers, damp shoes, and with his 4-ring oil-soaked shoulder boards attached, Lee made his way to the bridge.

"Permission to come on the Bridge, Captain?" Lee asked, following protocol to the letter, for now he was just a passenger.

Many faces on *Wilton's* bridge turned to look at him. A young Lt Cmdr. stepped forward to meet him, hand outstretched. "Hello, sir, I am Leech, welcome onboard."

"Thank you for stopping, Captain, how many of my crew did you manage to save?" Lee asked.

"We have one hundred and eight crew and four officers, Mr Watson, Jones, Vickers, and Backhouse. They are all down below, officers in the wardroom, seamen on the forward mess deck, it's a bit cramped down there!"

It felt like somebody had kicked him. Three quarters of his ships company were gone; what a waste! "With your permission, Captain, may I go and visit them?" Lee asked.

"Of course, messenger, show Captain Lee around the ship."

"Follow me, sir."

The telephone rang near the captain's chair, as he turned to answer it, Lee and the messenger left the bridge.

The *Wilton* was one of the new breed of powerfully armed escort destroyers, named after famous fox hunts in England. Being virtually brand new, Lee could smell the newness of the ship, which brought back more painful memories of the day he joined the newly built *Preston*. The messenger, Brown, by name, led the way to the forward mess deck. Upon entering, Lee was struck by the over powering smells of oil, blood, and cigarette smoke, which nearly made him retch again. He was happy to see the Coxswain, Buffer and Chief Yeoman, were among the survivors, and Timmins, his steward, was also there. But he was in a bad way, with a bandage over his eyes and was muttering incoherently. Lee slowly circulated the mess, making sure that he spoke to every member of his crew with a kind word. So many faces were missing. The alarm rattlers went off again, and some of the crew looked at the deckhead with fear in their eyes, and a few old hands carried on with their game of uckers. Lee stayed until the stand down was called, then made his way aft to the Wardroom.

Lee knocked on the Wardroom door. "Permission to enter," he called. Tradition again dictated had had to ask the occupants of the mess before entry.

"Enter," came the reply.

Stepping over the coaming, again he was assailed by the smell of cigarette smoke. Being an avid non-smoker, he hated that smell. His surviving officers were all sat together. Watson, the Executive officer, Backhouse the Navigator, and Vickers the Subby, stood up to greet him, but his Chief Engineer, Eric Jones, was lying on a couch, looking grey and drawn. Lee looked at Watson, who shook his head. Not good. All four were clothed in hand me downs, but were clean and unharmed. Mr Vickers went to the bar steward and collected four glasses of gin, then made a toast to *Preston*!

"Have you all been treated well?" Lee asked.

"Yes," they all replied. Lee stayed for a while talking and discussing what they have been through, and he asked them to make statements for the Board of Enquiry, that was sure to follow, regarding the loss of *Preston*. Operation Pedestal, the Malta convoy they were escorting, had lost a lot of good ships, and no doubt the Admiralty would want a full report.

It was dusk when Lee made his way back to the bridge. Leech was sat hunched in his chair, clearly exhausted. Lee stood nearby. "Captain, why don't you take a break. I can cover till you get back?"

Leech slowly turned to look at him, his face was grey and etched with fatigue. "Are you sure, sir? I could do with using the bathroom and a change of clothes."

"Of course, if anything happens, I will call you."

"Okay thanks, I won't be long, we are heading North by East speed sixteen knots, the convoy is ahead, and we are tail-end charley, we are at defence stations. Admiral Burrough transferred to the destroyer *Ashanti*, who is ahead, and the tanker *Ohio* is astern with two destroyers." With that Leech staggered from the bridge.

Brown the messenger stepped forward, "Cup of Kye sir," holding a steaming cup in his hands.

"Lovely, well-done, Brown." Brown turned away. The Captain had remembered his name! "No 1, I have the bridge; do you have anything urgent to do?"

Astern the night sky was lit up by gunfire, and the sound of explosions rumbled over the sea. The enemy were determined to sink that tanker. Ahead the convoy sailed in silence. Around midnight Leech returned to the bridge. "I am so sorry, sir, I fell asleep."

Lee smiled. "That's okay, John, you needed the rest, plus nothing has happened." They stood and talked for an hour, remembering past friends and laughed at 'runs ashore', then Lee retired to his bunk.

The alarm rattlers woke Lee. "Dawn Action stations, all hands to your action stations," a strong Geordie voice over the tannoy called. Lee dressed and slowly made his way to the bridge. Everybody was alert and scanning their lookout sectors.

Standing at the back of the bridge, he was joined by his No. 1 Andy Watson. "Morning, sir." Lee nodded.

A voice calls, "Dawn, sir."

"Very good, make a note in the log," Leech replies. "Radar... Bridge 20 aircraft to the North East."

"Very good, DCT... can you see them yet?" The silence drags on, as the Gunnery control officer in the Director Control Tower scans the sky for the small black dots. "Bridge... DCT got 'em Spitfires from Malta."

A cheer goes around the ship. The lifting of tension is palpable. The aircraft set themselves up into a protective circle over the convoy. Shortly, a flight of Beaufighter streak across the convoy, on their way to protect the stragglers.

Leech turns to Lee and beckons him forward. "Never seen that before, how many times have we wished for them!" They both nod and smile, maybe, just maybe, things are changing. For months the enemy had ruled the skies in the central Mediterranean basin; the navy had lost many good ships and men to these damn enemy aircraft.

As they approach Malta's Grand Harbour, the enemy has one last go at the convoy, swarms of Ju88's Ju87's and Me 110's scream down on the convoy. Every gun opens fire and the Spitfires swoop down onto the attacking enemy. The sky is filled with tracer bullets and exploding shells, diving planes, enemy and friendlies pass overhead, followed by a stream of explosions. Close enough that the gun batteries over the Grand Harbour join in, there is no restrictions on ammunition expenditure now. The sky is black with smoke from exploding shells. Lee looks over the Bridge screen at "A" gun and smiles as he sees his men manning the gun, shoulder to shoulder with *Wilton's* crew.

"Look out," someone screams, as a Me 110 fighter, strafes *Wilton* from bow to stern. Its four 20mm cannons ripping decks, bulkheads, ships boats and men apart. Leech is cut in two, his No 1 is lying crumpled in a corner, the navigator is wounded, signalmen and look outs are lying around the bridge in various unnatural poses. There is a small fire in the chart office, and an injured signalman is trying to put it out. Lee looks again at 'A' gun. Its crew is wiped out, bits of bodies and gore cover the mounting.

Most of the gun's crew have been killed. Looking up at the DCT, he sees blood leaking through bullet holes in the tower's thin sides. It drips onto the bridge deck, as if the tower itself is wounded. He looks around the bridge, by some miracle he and Watson are the only ones left standing, although Watson has a wounded arm.

The ship is slowly turning to Starboard; the voice tubes and phones are all asking for advice. Lee steps forward. "Okay, No 1, if you are up to it, we have a ship to run?"

"Damage control parties report, Doctor to the Bridge, Engine room, give me an update, *Preston's* crew report to your stations!" The orders flow.

The steering compartment is a bloody mess. The 20mm shells had ripped through the thin steel and decimated the men in there. The helmsman had died with his hand on the ships wheel, that's why she was slowly turning to starboard. *Preston's* Cox'n stepped across the coaming into this slaughter house and took charge. "Cox'n at the wheel sir, course, please?" he asked, as he gently removed the dead man's hand.

The ship slowly came back into action. The death toll was appalling; had it not been for *Preston's* rating and officers, the ship could have been lost. Watson set the crew to clearing up. Bodies were placed in hammocks and prepared for burial, although Alan suspected they would be taken off once in harbour. The *Wilton's* young crew were in a state of shock, and stood around transfixed, but if it wasn't for *Preston's* crew, who led the clean-up, *Wiltons* crew would have given in.

Wilton followed closely behind the cargo ships; they enter the 'safe' haven of The Grand Harbour of Malta. Alan is shocked at the bomb damage that the Three Cities have endured. The harbour walls are thronged with cheering Maltese and service men, all happy to see the arrival of 'The Santa Maria convoy'. Onboard the ships that have arrived, there will be just enough provisions and supplies to last the next six months. If *Ohio* can also get in, they will have enough fuel to go on the offensive. Lee managed to send a signal to all concerned about the *Wilton's* Captain and crew, and as they entered the Grand Harbour, he was instructed to remain in command and bring the ship back to Gibraltar. The dead were landed, and frantic refuelling and ammunition stocks were replaced and *Wilton* leaves her berth and turns in the harbour, desperately trying to avoid the many sunken wrecks that litter the place.

As he looks over to the Naval Dockyard, he can just make out the blackened and twisted stern of *Preston's* 'chummy' ship, *Jersey*, damaged many months ago. Across from the dockyard, the aircraft carrier, *HM*S *Illustrious,* listing to port with huge holes in her sides, and with smoke issuing from her flight deck. Pummelled by Stuka dive-bombers, she is tied up, for all to see, her damage clearly visible. She would sail again, but her damage and crew losses are grievous.

As they leave harbour, the broken tanker *Ohio* is ushered into port. Three destroyers are tied to the battered hull. They are determined to get her in. Her badly damaged hull so low in the water, you could have put your hand in the water from the main deck. Three huge gaping holes in her hull let the water surge in and out, and the smouldering wreckage of two enemy aircraft perched on her deck. When the watching crowd saw this, they lapsed into silence. The crowds on the battlements then start cheering, as every ship salutes their gallant efforts. Lee contacts the Admiral on the Talk Between Ships (TBS for short). "Sir, we have no confidential books, cyphers or charts. Can you contact me with either TBS or flag signals, and can you tell the Admiralty what's going on?"

"Hello, Alan, good to hear you are safe and in charge of *Wilton*, follow 'Father', and we will sort it out at Gib!"

As they leave harbour, the destroyers fan out and increase to twenty-five knots for the return to Gibraltar, *Wilton* follows *Ashanti* closely. Overhead an escort of Spitfires circle. They continue west. As they approach Skerki Bank Narrows, they proceed in line ahead, for these are dangerous waters. Beaufighters had replaced the Spitfires as escorts. But now, at extreme range, they also have to turn back. Once again, an Italian Air Force SM79 (Hunchback) starts to shadow the group. Through the night *Wilton* follows the blue stern light of the ship in front, he dared not lose sight of it. The following morning as dawn action stations are about to stand down. A mixed force of JU88, and SM79 make a high-level bombing run on the ships, there is a near miss on the destroyer *Melville*, but no further damage is reported.

A short while later, 'Force H' hove into view. They are here to escort the destroyers back to Gib. Admiral Somerville (Force H commander) orders the destroyers to sail between the 'Force H' ships, where they are cheered by every passing warship. Apart from the continuing shadowing enemy aircraft there are no further attacks on the force. Operation Pedestal is completed.

They berth at the drydock wall in Gibraltar Harbour, where *Wilton* is taken in hand for emergency repairs, the various ships then depart for other assignments. Lee is ordered to attend a board of enquiry into the loss of *Preston*, and the events leading up to taking command of *Wilton*, at Admiralty House. Lee, along with Watson, Backhouse and Jones attends the enquiry, seated across from him is Admiral Burrough, Admiral Somerville and two other Captains. Alan defends himself and produces the statements made by his officers regarding the loss of *Preston*. *Wilton's* No 1 also is present to give evidence on the attack on his ship. It takes almost five hours of evidence, seated in borrowed clothes, in the sweltering heat of high summer in the Mediterranean.

The results are in. The loss of *Preston* was down to the actions of the enemy, i.e., the laying of an unknown minefield across the path of the convoy. As for the command of *Wilton*, Lee and his officers are to be commended in their actions to prevent the possible loss of one of His Majesty's warships.

The court is dismissed, but Alan, Watson and Jones are asked to stay behind. In the more informal meeting in the courtroom, a steward brings in cool lemonade for everyone.

Admiral Summerville starts: "Alan, your actions in command of *Preston* have been exemplary, and we are recommending you for the DSO. Your recommendations for awards for your crew have been approved, without reservation. After survivors leave, you will take command of the cruiser, *Stockport*, the previous instructions to join *Invincible* are cancelled. You will be joined by other units, and you will form a strike force for operations against the Japanese.

"Mr Watson, you also are to be commended for your actions and a DSC is on its way, you have a choice of what every you want. Mr Jones, Your dedication to your department is above reproach, also a DSC is being awarded, however you are to return to the UK, your time at sea is over; you are to take command of the *HMS Sultan* in Portsmouth."

He continues, "Gentlemen, will you take *Wilton* back to Plymouth, for a new Captain? I have nobody available here, and it will get you all home quicker. Also take *Preston's* crew with you?"

A joint "Yes, sir" reaches his ears.

Later in The Crown and Anchor in Main St., the three officers are sat having a drink and discussing their futures. Eric Jones had recovered from the sinking, but was happy to be going ashore, as he said, "It's a young man's war now."

Lee laughed. "Never mind, Eric, you will have all those young engineers to train, that will keep you very busy!" Andy Watson has intimated that he wants to serve with Lee in the *Stockport*, which made him very humble. The door opened and a group of sailors entered, Lee could see they were *Preston* men. They spotted their Captain straight away and rushed over to great them. Soon the little table was groaning under the weight of beers and shots of whiskey and gin. Everybody was in a happy mood. After all they were all going home. The Cox'n and Buffer and Chief Yeoman have all said they would like to serve with the Captain again, along with a lot of the sailors.

The following morning, repairs were temporarily completed. The remnants of the night were still lingering amongst the destroyer trots and piers. Berthed at the South Mole, HMS *Repulse's* sea boat was being hoisted at the run, the falls creaking through wooden blocks until halted by the stentorian 'high enough'. Officers, signalmen and lookouts were waiting, motionless and silent on *Wilton* bridge.

Ian Carrie the Chief Yeoman speaks, "Proceed in execution of previous orders, Executive to follow."

Lee nods, and speaks, "Ring on main engines. Obey telegraphs."

In response telegraphs whirred in the wheelhouse, an answering bell is heard from the engine room. "Main engines rung on, sir." the Cox'n replies up the voice pipe. "Execute signal, sir."

"Very well. Let go forward, let go aft, hold on the springs, slow astern starboard." The f'c'sle and quarterdeck men haul in the berthing wires which slap briefly against the hull. The turbines began to revolve with a high-pitched whine; the propellors gripping the water, as the ship moved backwards on the spring, straining against it until the bows swung away from the jetty. "Let go spring, half ahead port," Lee spoke.

Wilton headed for the harbour entrance, commencing her journey home. She is to join a Liverpool bound convoy as an extra escort. Once clear of the 'Pillars of Hercules', *Wilton* entered the Atlantic, which greeted them with storm force six winds, after a 10,000-ton cruiser, a 1,000-ton destroyer rolled and pitched, a very uncomfortable ride. Thankfully the enemy left them alone, and six days later, *Wilton* detached and headed for Plymouth.

Once the ship was tied up in Plymouth dockyard, she was handed over to the shipyard's custody. Lee and the rest of *Preston's* survivors held a church service, at St. Nikolas in *HMS Drake*., to thank the lord for bringing them home safe. They then dispersed to take the tram or bus to the railway station and their loved ones. The wooden hand carts were loaded with the sailor's kit and were pushed, 'groaning' up the hill to Plymouth Railway station. Lee headed home to the small cottage in Eggbuckland, where his wife Sheila and three children lived. Glad at last to immerse himself in family life.

Chapter 2

A few weeks later, Lee had received his orders, and after saying goodbye to his beloved family, he was to proceed to the Admiralty in London for instructions, then to join *Stockport* in Glasgow. First, though he was taking the overloaded wartime train from Plymouth to Central London. It was crammed with uniforms from every branch of the armed services. French, Dutch, Poles and a few Americans were also packed aboard. The journey took forever. Constant stops and shunted into sidings, Alan watched fascinated as fully loaded freight trains rushed past, carrying ammunition, trucks and tanks. He remembered his time in Russia and wondered if any of these were headed that way. He shuddered at the thought of another Arctic convoy. Eventually, and with relief, he left the train in London. Hailing one of the few taxis around, he presented himself at the Admiralty building.

Standing in the foyer, in his brand-new uniform, resplendent with his medals proudly displayed for everyone to see, he was a warrior come for more instructions. He waited in an adjoining room for a few minutes. A smart looking, but harassed Flag Lieutenant entered, and ushered him into another room. Lee smiled.

Why is it that all flag lieutenants looked haggard? He was so glad he never raised to that lofty position! Admiral Wake-Walker sat at his table. It was littered with signal pads, lists and charts. Acknowledging Lee's salute, he started the briefing. "Captain Lee, welcome, you will be appointed to command Force 'Y'. You will have a small force of ships *Stockport*: one heavy cruisers, two light cruisers, four destroyers and an escort Carrier. Your role will be to search out and destroy Japanese shipping in and around the Dutch East Indies, and the Australian coast. You are to assist with the American fleet in that area. But you take your orders from us. Understand?"

"Sir."

"But first I want *Stockport* to be part of a fast convoy to Malta. They are in desiderate need of more food, twenty-millimetre gun barrels and anti-aircraft shells. You will sail in two weeks' time. Your orders will be forwarded to you onboard *Stockport*. Questions?"

They carried on with timings, supply etc. for another two hours.

While Lee was at the Admiralty, in the John Browns yard in Glasgow, two happy sailors were heading back to *Stockport* with a rolling motion, curtesy of the local 'heavy' beer. As they neared the ship, they were aware of a few dockyard workers lined up at the dockyard latrines. Now, the toilet block did not have flushing toilets, it had a constant flow of water from the River Clyde, which took the 'waste' out and back into the Clyde. An efficient but unhygienic practice. Leading Seaman Steve De Asha was one of *Stockport* characters and a survivor of the *Preston* sinking. Along with his oppo Steve Dann, from another seamen's mess. They decided to have a little fun! Finding a plank of waste wood, they put some wood chippings and oily rags on the plank, set fire to it, and launched it into the inlet pipe for the latrines. They then scampered of to a safe distance to await the results! It didn't take long, as a cacophony of yells shattered the evening air, as the flaming 'boat' made its way through the toilets on its way to the sea. Six angry dockers emerged, adjusting their dress, as two figures disappeared into the darkness, laughing hysterically. *Stockport* 1 *Workers* 0!

One day later, Lee stands on the brow of his new ship, taking the salute that welcomes onboard a new Captain. Lt Cmdr. Andy Watson steps forward with a huge smile on his face and his hand held out. "Welcome onboard, sir."

The next few days were a blur of meetings, paperwork, and planning. His new command, the light cruiser, HMS *Stockport*, was the first Town class built for the Royal Navy, a near sister of his beloved *Preston*. She had been in the Norway campaign but had to return due to problems with her turbines. Once in dry dock in Glasgow, she was bombed by the Luftwaffe, and a major fire gutted the aft part of the ship. So much water was pumped onboard to fight the fire, that she sank on her starboard side. It had taken two years to repair and refit the ship. *Stockport* was now ready for war again: her six-inch guns had been upgraded, her four-inch battery had extra armoured crew shelters added, her light anti-aircraft weapons now feature twenty mm. Oerlikons, forty mm. Bofors and two pdrs. Pom Poms, a formidable battery. The masts and superstructure were festooned with Radar Aerials — how Lee had wished for these earlier in the war. Because he had been held up in London, Andy Watson had overseen a lot of the fitting out, so knew the ship intimately, so Lee had to rely on him a lot. The ships Engineer was Commander Ray Arnold RN, a no-nonsense man from Derby. Lee had had a few meetings with him, and he seemed on top of his game, but he missed the steady hand of Eric Jones, *Preston's* Chief Engineer. Fault fixing and trials took a few more days, but finally he was ready to sail to Scapa Flow, for work up. The hurried work up in Scapa lasted one week. *Stockport* then sailed south to Glasgow to refuel and load the precious parts and food needed by the island of Malta. Once loaded she moved to the 'Tail 'o' the Bank' and anchored to await the rest of the convoy. While at anchor, Watson had the crew on endless drills and exercises. A sprinkling of experienced crew had joined, but there was a lot of new 'baby' sailors that needed a lot more training.

The following morning, they sailed. It was a cold miserable day with low cloud and an angry swell. As was normal, two minesweepers led the ships out of the Clyde, where the Local Escort Group was doing an anti-submarine sweep. In line astern, followed, the fast minelayers, *Apollo, Ariadne*, then *Stockport* and *Exeter*, and the AA cruiser, *Ceres* and *Capetown*, leaving their escorts behind, they increased speed to twenty-eight knots and headed south down the Irish Sea. As they exited the western approaches, the sky darkened even more, and the force headed into a gale. The seas rose and the ships started to pitch and role. The two 'C' class cruisers taking it badly, soon they had to slow down to prevent storm damage. The Fast Minelayers with *Stockport* and *Exeter* forged on. Entering the Bay of Biscay the storm deepened, and the 'Bay' did what it did best — ferociously attacked the ships. The seas flowed over the decks, lockers and other equipment was swept overboard. The wind howled through the rigging. Watson did a turn around the ship. Nearly all of the new crew members were incapacitated with sea sickness, bodies in every nook and cranny retching into buckets or overboard. The few experienced sailors having to take over the sick rating duties, obviously should little or no sympathy to their erstwhile shipmates. 'If you couldn't take a joke, you shouldn't have joined' was heard many times around the ship.

As they passed Ferrol, in Spain, the seas abated, and blue sky appeared overhead. Both *Ceres* and *Capetown* were reporting a shortage of fuel. So, the Admiral in *Ariadne* ordered them to enter Lisbon, Portugal, for fuel. The other ships slowed down and waited outside. *Ceres* and *Capetown* had been built at the end of WWI, although they were powered by fuel oil, their operational range had been limited to working in the North Sea against the German High Seas Fleet. In the thirties, they had been converted into Anti-Aircraft cruisers, with the main armament changed to High Angle guns, and with a modest increase in fuel bunkerage. Although handy ships, their lack of range was problematic. A few hours later, they resumed their journey to Gibraltar, at a slightly slower speed, so as to pass the Straights during darkness, to avoid the German spies operating in Southern Spain. Unfortunately, they had to pass through a Spanish Fishing fleet, so the secret was out.

Berthed at various points in Gibraltar Harbour, the cruiser, topped up fuel, and additionally took aboard members of the RAF and Army for delivery to Malta. Also waiting them were the Fast transport SS *Clan Campbell*, and SS *Clan Duncan*. These were packed full of essential and much needed equipment and supplies. They were also veterans of many Malta supply runs over the past two years and had managed to survive! The eight Captains met in a meeting room in the Rock to discuss the upcoming operation. Another five Captains later joined them; these would be their destroyer escorts. The following evening as the sun was setting, the whole force left the safety of Gibraltar Harbour and headed west out into the Atlantic. Again, this was to deceive the watching spies. Once totally dark and before the moon rose above the horizon, they turned around, increased speed and re-entered the Mediterranean. Unfortunately, they were spotted by the much-delayed Algeciras to Morocco ferry. So, again the secret was out.

They settled down to a speed of twenty knots, just short of the transport's maximum. Through the night they sped along; the sky was clear, the stars in stark relief, and the seas was calm. By sunrise, they were well into their journey, it was beautiful day, the sky was cloudless, and the sea remained calm. *Stockport's* ships company went about their business, sea sickness forgotten for the moment. At lunch time, the radar sets were reporting aircraft to the North and East, obviously looking for the convoy. Having survived many air attacks in the past, Lee kept his men at defence stations, having them at Action Stations, causing unnecessary fatigue, so letting his men rest as much as possible. One of the destroyers, *Maori*, reported a submarine contact, and turned in a welter of foam to attack. *Stockport* went to action stations. Moment later, ten waterspouts were spotted rising in *Moari's* wake, followed by ten percussions, felt through seaboots as her depth charges exploded. Because most of his crew had not been in action before, he had one of the bridge messengers inform the ships company over the tannoy on what was going on, so when they heard the depth charges going off, they would understand.

With the ships company watching *Moari*, nobody was looking ahead. Ian Carrie the Chief Yeoman spotted an aircraft on the horizon and called out. 'Aircraft in sight, dead ahead.'

'DCT... Bridge aircraft in sight bearing green 010, looks like an SM79, sir."

"Well done, Chief. No 1, please tell your lookouts to watch their sectors, not *Moari*! DCT, if it comes in range, open fire!" Lee was angry. They nearly missed it; he must wake these lookouts up. Andy Watson was seething. He should have seen the lookouts weren't watching their sectors; he was angry with himself for failing Lee. It would not happen again.

Out of range the 'snooper' circled the convoy. Just before the sun set, a mixed force of Italian high level and torpedo bombers attacked out the 'dark' side of the sky. A brief engagement results in two bombers and a torpedo bomber shot down, with only a near miss on *Ashanti*, one of the escorting destroyers. Soon, they would have to reduce speed, deploy paravanes and break formation and go to two columns line astern, as they approached the dreaded Skerki Bank, the resting place of many brave ships and men. *Stockport's* radar began picking up small fast-moving MAS Boats; they were lethal in these confined waters. *Stockport* hauled out of line a fired three full six-inch gun broadsides in the direction of the MAS Boats. This obviously had a desired effect, on the radar repeater screens on the bridge, some echoes were seen to fade, as some of the boats sank, and the remainder were watched as they withdrew in the direction of Pantelleria. Smiles of satisfaction were seen on the bridge.

As dawn broke, they cleared the Narrows, as in previous times, the ships increased speed, and would have headed southeast, to increase the distance away from the airfields on Sicily. As *Apollo* hauled aboard her starboard paravane, they found a torpedo entangled in the wires. Therefore, she had to slow down and stop as her crew cut the torpedo loose, as it swung precariously close to the ships side. Then as quickly as she could, go astern dropping the unwanted 'package' into the deep blue water. Once clear she quickly rejoined the convoy. But this time, on Lee's insistence they kept a steady course due east, towards Malta. As the distance to Malta narrowed, *Stockport's* radar screens showed activity to the south as enemy aircraft, desperately searched for the convoy on what had been there 'usual' course. Eventually, around mid-afternoon, they were spotted. A passing He111 reported their position. Fortunately, the time they had remained unobserved had been put to good use. The ships crews had rested and fed. Again, changed into clean underwear, ammunition bins reloaded, guns checked and recalibrated, and the upper deck crews wearing their anti-flash gear stood ready. Soon the radar was reporting massed aircraft formations heading their way. It was a mix of dive-bombers and torpedo planes. Having recovered their paravanes, all ships were free to manoeuvre independently and at speed.

The German aircraft fell upon them with ferocity. Soon the air was filled with the scream of aero engines, the crump of exploding bombs, the bark of four-inch-high angle guns. Lee was watching the sky, and as an enemy plane started to attack *Stockport*, he would order a course and speed change. The noise was terrific, the steady pom pom sound from the 2pdrs and Bofors guns, and the clatter as spent shell cases landed on the steel decks. *Stockport's* shooting was poor, this was, after all, a new ships company. Lee thought if we survive this, he will have the crew drilled more intensely.

Forty minutes later, to Watson it felt a lot longer, the enemy withdrew. Unseen by the lookouts, *Sikh,* one of the escorting destroyers, had been hit by multiple bombs and had disintegrated in a loud explosion. So intense had been the attack, Lee had not noticed *Sikh's* demise. *Capetown* had been hit by a bomb that destroyed her aft gun positions but could still keep up. *Clan Campbell* had been hit by a Stuka dive-bomber, that, then crashed onto her foredeck; its burnt out skeletal remains there for all to see. Lee sat in his bridge chair. He was exhausted and felt weak — how many more attacks could he handle, he thought. The Chief yeoman, Carrie, passed him a cup of coffee, with a large helping of rum in it, that settled his nerves a bit.

The night came to them: his crew went about their business, cleaning up the ship, replacing ammunition, having something to eat, and of course sleep when and where you could. Lee left the bridge to go to his day cabin, all around the bridge and upper decks, he could make out the sleeping forms of his crew. A voice out of the night, "Evening, sir, do you need anything?" peering into the darkness he spotted De Asha, one of his ships 'characters'.

"Thanks, Hooky, just having a walk, carry on."

"Yes sir, good night, sir."

Dawn brought a tired Lee onto the bridge, the ship was called to dawn action stations, and anxious eyes scanned the horizon. The peace was shattered. "Radar... Bridge ten aircraft approaching from the east." An audible groan went up from the crew. "Masthead... Bridge ten Beaufighters approaching Red 010."

Lee spoke, "Relax everyone, it's our escort from Malta," and loud sigh was heard.

Under the protection of the Beaufighters and later Spitfires, they were not attacked again. *Apollo*, *Ariadne* and *Capetown* increased speed and headed for Malta. They would be unloaded and be clear of the harbour as the rest of the convoy arrived. As *Stockport* and the rest closed the harbour's entrance *Apollo* and *Ariadne* had finished offloading and were heading out for Alexandria on further orders. As they entered Lee looked to the port side and could just make out the wreck of *Ohio*. The tanker that they had recently fought to deliver to Malta desperately needed fuel. Eight hours later, the warships were offloaded, and refuelled and departed Malta. The two fast transports remained to carry on offloading. The cruisers and destroyers headed west at twenty-eight knots, glad to be going home. Unmolested, they all reached Gibraltar safely, where they dispersed and went about their business. *Stockport* heading north for Scapa Flow, and more gunnery training. Lee retired to his bunk and slept the sleep of the dead.

At Scapa, Lee took some leave, he was exhausted, while the usual rounds of exercises and drills, shaped *Stockport's* crew into fighting efficiency. Once the workup was completed, the force began to assemble, It included: *Kent* a county class cruiser, 2 anti-aircraft cruisers *Bellona* and *Dido*, 4 brand new, "L" class destroyers *Lavish*, *Lively*, *Lightning* and *Lookout*, powerfully armed with twin 4.7 in Dual Purpose turrets. HMS *Georgic* a Cargo liner that had been converted into an escort carrier, bigger than the escort carriers now arriving from the USA on lend lease, faster at 22 knots and able to carry more aircraft. She was commanded by an ex-Fleet Air Arm pilot, Commander Pat Byrne RN. He had spent many years developing aircraft tactics at the Admiralty and was as keen as mustard to try them out. Lee was very happy he was with them. He had also been supplied with a tanker, the *RFA Blue Rover*, as well as an ammunition and stores ship *Empire Brecon*, with their own escort of two sloops, *Magpie* and *Wren*. These last four would meet him in Trincomalee in Ceylon. The strike force had specially been selected for their powerful AA batteries, for the Japanese air forces were formidable foes.

Mid November, and the ships set sail for Gibraltar. Once in mid Atlantic, Lee set too, making the ships companies, practice various action scenarios. Watson also had *Stockport's* ships company on various drills. They organized a series of aircraft fly pasts, where three Avengers flew in a straight line at a set speed and altitude, towing a banner on the end of 500 feet of line. The ship's gun crews could then fire live ammunition at the banner to practice their gunnery skills. All did not go well at the start, and after a few minutes, one of the aircraft was heard on the radio, "*Dido* this is *Tango* 3, please inform your gunners, that I am towing the bloody banner not pushing it!" Although amusing it did have the effect of improving the accuracy. Nobody wanted to be responsible for shooting down one of our own aircraft. After which

Georgic had her Avenger aircraft on a search pattern around the force, keeping a watchful eye on their surroundings, her Wildcat fighters were up also, doing practice intercepts and giving the various ships gunners important aerial recognition work and target practice. Lee watched the carrier with an inquisitive eye, but they seemed to know what they were doing.

Stood at the back of the bridge, the Chief Yeoman CPO Ian Carrie was content, having served, and been a fellow survivor with Lee on *Preston*, he was happy to sign on again with him in *Stockport*. He looked around at his young signalmen, all bar two, were straight out of the training school, and were as green as grass. But they all appeared to be pulling their weight. Still, he will keep his eye on them all. Looking at the back of Lee's head he smiled. 'Yes one of the better skippers,' he yelled. "Palmer, what is *Bellona* saying?" Ah keep them on their toes.

Crossing the Bay of Biscay, the radar sets picked up an aerial target approaching from the East. *Georgic* scrambled two fighters, which went snarling off to intercept. From the radio repeater on the bridge, Lee and the rest of the bridge party could listen in on the intercept. "Red Leader to Mother, we can see the target, it's a FW 200 Condor, setting up to intercept over." Silence. "Red 2, watch out for that tail gunner." The sound of machine gun fire could be heard as he opened fire. "Red 2, John, are you OK?" Two more fighters were launched from *Georgic* that raced off in the direction of the fight.

"Red Leader from Red 2, am OK but I have a few more holes in the cockpit!"

The sound of machine guns could be heard again. "Red 2, head back to mother, I have set its port engines on fire, I don't think it will last long."

Again silence, and a few minutes later. "Red leader to Mother splash one Condor! Am returning." Cheering broke out on the bridge.

"Chief Yeoman, send a message to *Lavish*; ask her to go see if there are any survivors." He doubted it, at this temperature in the Atlantic, they would not last long. The ships signal lamp stared clacking away. *Lavish* turned in a welter of spray and shot of at speed towards the downed aircraft. Moments later the damaged Red 2 landed, followed by the leader. "Bunts signal *Georgic,* well done." First blood to Force 'Y'.

An hour later *Lavish* hove in sight, her signal lamp flashing away. "No Survivors, sir," read out by the signalman.

Force 'Y' slowed down near the entrance to the Mediterranean, and he sent *Lavish* and *Lively* and *Dido* into Gibraltar for fuel. When they returned, he sent the other two destroyers and *Bellona* for fuel. He was blessed, *Stockport* and *Kent*, had been built with cruising in mind so they had a range of 10,000 miles, so did not need to refuel often; however it was always better to refuel when he could. With the force fuelled, they increased speed to 20 knots and headed for Freetown. The sea turned a deeper blue, and the wind became warmer as they headed south.

The crew shifted into Tropical White uniforms, and so many sickly white limbs began to appear. The Cox'n went around the ship, giving out dire warnings for any rating who gets himself sunburn. As they approach Freetown, Alan has an idea. "No 1, ask the Buffer and Cox'n to come to the bridge."

Later, "Gentlemen, we have a lot of baby sailors onboard, I would suggest that a visit from King Neptune and his court might be possible in a few days." This met with everybody's approval. Lee and Watson remembered back to *Preston's* 'crossing the line ceremony' and smiled, but tinged with sadness, so many were now perished.

"Message from *Lookout* sir!"

"Go ahead."

"Having problems with my steering engine, sir."

"Bugger, OK, Chief send a message to Naval Officer in Charge Freetown, ask him for urgent dockside assistance for *Lookout* from the Kissy Dockyard in Freetown." He did not want to spend too much time in Freetown, and the Dockyard did not have a large capacity for repairs, but if they can't fix it, *Lookout* will have to stay here. "No 1, limited leave only, I don't want to spend much time in this port!"

"Aye sir!"

Its reputation for hungry mosquitos was well known in the fleet. After *Preston* fight with the two German ships, she had to call in Freetown for repairs. The *Preston*'s crew were tormented by these little flying monsters.

Once they were all anchored in the roadstead, they refuelled, as fast as the elderly tanker would allow. *Lookout* went alongside the rickety pier and some engineers came onboard to look at the problem. Ray Arnold also went to see *Lookout's* problem and to try and assist. As soon as the ships had anchored the message had got around, and each ship was hit by a cloud of tiny buzzing parasites. Nobody stayed on the upper decks unless they had to be there, and all sorts of strange garb was seen on the unfortunate sailors who had to be out there. "Officer of the Watch, *Lookout* signalling, repairs will take another five hours."

"Very good, acknowledge."

"Messenger, go down to the Captain's day cabin and tell him."

"Sir." Jenkins the messenger scampered off, glad to be off the upper decks. Born in the slums of East Manchester, he had left school with a limited education, but learned how to fight and survive in the dark alleyways and ginnels around his home. At fourteen he began working at the Moston Coal Mine, where his dad was Chief Electrician, but he hated it. He liked the electrical work but detested being underground. It was becoming very obvious that the war was coming. Out with his mates one day, and on a whim, he walked into the Navy recruiting office in Manchester, and joined up. Hoping to become an electrician like his dad, but the navy had other ideas, so he was sent to the Seaman Branch, at *Ganges*, he loved every minute of the training! This was his life now.

Now he was on the *Stockport*, heading to the Far East, how his life had changed.

Aft into Officer Territory, he was soon at the Captain's door. The Marine Guard looked down at him. "What do you want?"

"Message from the OOW for the Captain."

"Wait." Knock on the door and the Marine calls, "Messenger for you, sir."

"Enter."

Jenkins stepped across the coaming, and with wide eyes looked around the Captain's day cabin; he had never been in here before, and it looked like a palace. *Stockport* had been built between the wars and had been fitted out as a Flagship for cruising on foreign stations, so the cabin was made to display Britain at its best. Most of the opulent fittings had been stripped away, but it still looked great.

"Yes, Jenkins." He was taken aback; the Captain remembered his name and he had only met him twice! He relayed his message. "Thank you, Jenkins, how are you finding life onboard *Stockport*?" he asked.

They had a moment or two of pleasant conversation before Jenkins was dismissed. Off he scampered to tell his mates all about it. Being in such a hurry to leave, he fell over the door coaming, right in front of a grinning Marine. On his way back to the bridge he called at the canteen, where he had had a quick cup of tea, and rubbed his sore shins.

Seven hours later *Lookout* was ready to proceed. "No 1, let's get underway." Soon they were heading out of the river estuary, glad to leave the Mossies behind! The very next day the ships were ready for King Neptune's visit. Once again Andy Watson would be Neptune. The Buffer would lead the 'Polliwogs' to roundup recalcitrant crew members. The dunking pool and the washing pool were ready in the port waist, and the festivities lasted a couple of hours, then an impromptu party until darkness fell, fuelled by illicitly stored rum and bottles of beer. There were a few sore heads and bodies the next morning! Andy Watson let them alone this day but was back the following day with his drills and exercises.

The temperature was stifling, but with the breeze it was acceptable, apart from the engine and boiler rooms. The engineer Arnold had put the watches in the engine and boiler rooms on thirty mins on, thirty mins off to combat the heat. The ship during its refit had been fitted with a rudimentary air conditioning, which made a great difference inside these steel rooms. The further south they went the sea turned into a deep magenta colour. Next stop was Capetown — here *Lookouts* repairs could be checked and the crews given brief leave. A few minor faults had shown up on the cruise down, so the Royal Dockyard could sort them out. More Admiralty Orders and some extra radio operators joined the ship. The liberty men were assembled on the quarterdeck, where the Cox'n was laying down the law about the local women, and the consequences on coming back onboard with a dose of Venereal Disease, and a visit to the 'Rose Garden', which led to a charge of 'self-inflicted injury'. These threats didn't stop the revelry as the sailors trouped ashore.

Three days later, they sailed for Mombasa in Kenya. Now they would be on a war footing, extra lookouts have been posted and the ship was at defence stations. Lee was sat in his bridge chair, going through some paperwork that had been passed to him. Something moved in the corner of his peripheral vision! Looking closely, he spotted a small rangy mongrel terrier dog on the f'c'sle, with a heavily tattooed Leading seaman chasing after it! "No1, we appear to have a guest onboard!"

"I can see it, Leading Seaman De Asha, report to the bridge."

A few moments later a chastened Leading seaman arrived on the bridge with the puppy under his arm. No 1 spoke, "Well, hooky, who's this?"

"Sir, this is Nipper, picked him up in Cape Town, being treated badly by some locals, sir. I thought the new sailors could do with a ship's mascot. I hope it's all right, sir," De Asha spoke.

Watson guessed there was more to that story, but let it pass. He turned and looked at Lee, who smiled and nodded his head. Looking back at the Leading Seaman and wishing he had thought about it! "Hooky, have Ordinary Seaman Nipper entered onto the ship's books, draw rations from your mess, and any 'Little presents' will be your responsibility!"

"Yes sir, thank you, sir," as he scurried away. Nipper became a member of No 2 Seamans mess and had an ongoing campaign with the rat population on board, and his action station was on 'A' gun, along with his messmates. He only ever barked when his gun was fired! De Asha had befriended Jenkins when he came onboard. He kept his eye on his young 'oppo', helping him through the ways of the navy. Teaching him how to avoid getting caught by the Crushers! The run ashore in Cape Town had been Jenkins first time on foreign soil. Being young and naive he soon fell victim to the local criminals. Trapped in a back alley by a grim looking bunch of locals, he was made to hand over his watch and all the money he had. He was then presented with the mangy looking dog, Nipper. The shout *'Stockport's* on me' startled the gang, as De Asha and 20 crewmates stampeded into the alley. Fists flew, along with belt buckles and knuckle dusters, six local men lay in the dust, bleeding and torn. De Asha retrieved Jenkins's watch and money, and a few extra pounds from the unconscious men, and the *Stockport* crew left in a hurry, along with Nipper, who ran alongside them, his tail wagging furiously!

East then north, they sped up the Mozambique Channel at 20 knots, *Georgic's* Avenger aircraft out ahead looking for potential foes. On their port side could just be made out the wreck of the tanker *Africa Shell*, sunk by the German raider *Graf Spee*, and a reminder for everyone to keep a sharp lookout. As they pass Beira, they have a submarine scare, which turns out to be a shoal of fish, which was depth charged by *Lightning*. Ships boats were sent to collect the dead fish, and fish supper was on the menu for the whole force. A nice change in their diet. Days later they arrive at Mombasa entering Port Reitz opposite Old Mombasa. They refuel yet again and take onboard more supplies. The NOIC Mombasa is waiting for the force to arrive, for he has more instructions and intelligence info for Lee. Eight hours later they left Mombasa. They head due East heading straight for the Addu Atoll, also known as Port 'T' — Britain's secret naval base.

Once they enter the Lagoon, the heat hits them like a furnace. Lee can see the construction of the new airfield on their port side to be called Gan, and the growing number of ships that are starting to make up the Far East Fleet. They follow the same ritual: refuel, collect stores and collect the ships mail. Soon they were on the move again. As they passed through the boom, Lee overheard a conversation between two of the lookouts. De Asha was quietly talking to Jenkins. "Cor, here we go, leaving this paradise, Scapa with Palm trees, nothing 'er, and nothing to do!" Lee smiled. Trust 'Jack' to name it.

They headed onwards towards their destination: the fleet anchorage at Trincomalee in Ceylon. Lee had ordered that the search patrol aircraft look further out and all around for there was a known Japanese force in the Indian Ocean. The weather now started to deteriorate; the sea began long steady rollers and the blue sky disappeared; dark thunder clouds appeared overhead. Soon the ships were pitching and rolling. It had got so bad that Lee ordered all aircraft back to the carrier. Lee watched as the aircraft started to recover. Eight had been sent out, so he had counted seven back, of the eighth there was no sign. *Georgic* had signalled it wanted to send out a search flight, but Lee refused — in this weather it did not make sense to risk more lives. The storm fell across them like a banshee. Huge waves and high winds battered the ships as they tried to make progress. The destroyers were taking it badly, so Lee ordered them to break formation and fend for themselves. *Georgic* was hit by a particular high sea, which swept two Avengers overboard, their lashings snapped like straws. For two days they fought the sea. On the third day it broke clear and blue, with the wind and sea moderating. What a change. Three of the destroyers and *Dido* had suffered storm damage but the fleet base at Trinco would soon fix them. Worryingly *Lookouts* steering engine was playing up again, the dockyard can look at that as well.

As they approached Ceylon, *Georgic* had flown off all her aircraft to a nearby airfield, RAF China Bay, where they could keep up their flying skills.

They entered the lush harbour, busy with shipping, and numerous harbour craft going about their business. The embarked Harbour Pilots, directing the ships to their allotted berths. Soon the ships companies were busy rigging awnings on the quarterdeck and waists, scuttles opened, wind scoops fitted, and heat descended on them all.

Chapter 3

Sub-lieutenant Steve Birch looked though his rain splattered windscreen. He was certain he had seen something down there. His observer Lt. Bill Smith and TAG Andy Bell were frantically looking out though the rain. The Avenger droned on. "Are you sure you saw something skipper," Bell asked.

"Yep, definitely a ship down there."

"We have a recall signal, Skip," Bell called out.

"OK a quick look, lower down, then we will scoot of home," Birch said.

Suddenly they emerged out from the rain squall, right over the top of a Japanese destroyer, the 'meatball' painted proudly on her forward turret roof.

"Oh god get us out of here, skipper," Smith called.

Birch pushed the engine throttle and added boost. As he yanked back on the control stick, the Avenger clawed at the sky, but it was too late — anti-aircraft shells exploded around them. "Andy, get a signal off too mother, tell them what we have found." Silence. Andy Bell was slumped in the turret, lifeless. Bill Smith reaches across for the radio controls, but the set was dead. Then the engine stopped, hit by a 37mm shell. Struggling with the controls,

Birch somehow managed a poor water landing, even if he did say so himself.

Pushing on the emergency hatch both he and Bill managed to get out. The stowed life raft did its job and started to inflate. They scrambled onboard as the aircraft took on a nose down posture and disappeared below the waves, taking Andy Bell with it.

Within minutes a Japanese launch was alongside them. The boat's crew roughly dragged them onboard, allowing the raft to drift away, where they proceeded to open fire on it, until it sank. Onboard the Jap destroyer, they were stripped naked on the deck, all their possessions were taken away. They were then taken into a storeroom where a bunch of Japanese officers started questioning them about their ship. When they wouldn't answer they started beating on them. This lasted for about three days until they could not take the punishment any longer. Very bravely they had refused to talk. As cold seawater was thrown over them repeatedly to revive them. Eventually, the tormentors tired of this game. They were then dragged onto the Quarterdeck, where they were used for bayonet and sword practice, before their lifeless bodies were dumped in the sea.

In Trincomalee harbour, with awnings spread to give some shade from the heat, the ships rested in a deep blue lagoon, surrounded by lush palm trees. One of the most idyllic spots on the planet, until very recently, untouched by war. That shock happened a few weeks ago when a Japanese task force descended on them. The remnants of a few sunk ships can still be seen in the shallower water. Little native craft scuttled around the harbour, like busy water beetles. Ships launches, and a few landing craft, known as 'Z' lighters, went about their business, keeping a wary eye on the Force flagship *Stockport*. *Georgic* planes were taking off and landing in an effort to increase the training of the new aircrews.

Lee was happy to see his supply ships and escorts all at anchor, one less worry! A conference had been called onboard the flagship, so all the Captains came onboard, firstly to hear what Lee had to say, and to get together over a gin or two. The first operation was to commence tomorrow, so all were eagerly awaiting the news. The two Royal Fleet Auxiliaries, *Empire Brecon* and *Blue Rover*, along with *Magpie* and *Wren*, would sail in the morning and head for a chart location near the Andaman Islands. There they will wait for the force to arrive. They will then refuel the Force and retire to another chart reference in the Indian Ocean, well off the main shipping lines — there they will again wait for the force to arrive. Lee will take the main force and cruise down the Burma coast looking for any enemy shipping. They would leave in two days' time so as to catch up with the slower supply ships.

Way to the south, in the Australian port of Melbourne, the eight thousand ton, three island tramp steamer the *SS Yorktown*, departed. She headed first west then northwest; her destination was Bombay in India, onboard was fifty-three seamen, seventeen D.E.M.S. Gunners and ten thousand tons of rice and mutton for the Indian army. At a sedately pace of eleven knots, this would be a three-week voyage. Leaving Melbourne, assembled on the poop deck, the gunners, under Bombardier George Butler, set about checking their ancient four-inch gun — it was built for use in WWI. With only twenty-five rounds of ammunition, they were not expected to fight a major action, just scare off any potential enemies. The sea was rough, and the steamer had a strange rolling motion that upset some of the gun crew.

Two days later, in Ceylon, the ships weighed anchor and proceeded slowly to the boom across the harbour. Three smokey old anti-submarine trawlers were the first to leave, searching for any hidden enemy, followed by the destroyers. The rest followed. Once clear of the shallow water they increased speed to 20 knots, with the aircraft rejoining *Georgic* after their time ashore. Lee was aware that he was three Avenger aircraft short, but at the moment there were none to be had. He was told that an aircraft transport was on its way with replacement, but there was no eta. The day was stunning, a gentle swell, warm wind and unlimited visibility. *Georgic* had already launched a search pattern of aircraft.

Lee spoke, "No 1, Action stations, damage in the forward stokers mess, and fire in the aft lobby, that will wake everybody up!" The Marine Bugler sounded the alarm. The ships company went about their business with a will. This made Lee smile. "There, getting better, No 1."

"Yes, sir, still a few more improvements yet."

Heading due east, they entered the Andaman Sea. Lee wanted to be about twenty miles off Cox's Bazar, in Burma, at daybreak. At 4.30 in the morning, they launched two search aircraft and four fighters for protection, to see if anything was at sea in the area. They reported back that two small coastal traders were at sea heading south, but nothing in the harbour. This was just what Lee was looking for. He recalled the aircraft. He did not want to let the Japs know there was a carrier in the area, and ordered *Lavish* and *lightning*, with *Dido* to attack with gunfire. He needed to 'blood' his force with an easy target. The two destroyers and the cruiser left station and headed for the last known sighting of the enemy ships. *Dido's* Captain, Bob Peel, took control and ordered the ships into line abreast to search.

One hour later *Lightning* reported smoke on the horizon. "Found 'em." In line ahead, *Lightning* leading, then *Dido* and *Lavish* taking up the rear, they closed the enemy ships. *Lightning* started to signal, "Heave too." This only brought a clouds of black smoke from the short fat funnel, and the merchant ships headed for shore. *Dido* fired across the leading ships bows. This had no effect. Open fire, came the order. *Lightning* and *Dido*, concentrated on the lead ship, with *Lavish* firing on the rear ship. It didn't last long. The lead ship, hit by 5.25 in and 4.7 in shells, slowed down and started to sink by the bow. The second one stopped after being hit once, and the small crew made a mad dash for the single lifeboat, the Japanese ensign being taken down by the crew, and thrown overboard as they left. *Lavish's* Captain made a quick decision and closed the wallowing merchant ship and sent a fully armed boarding party across.

Upon boarding, some sailors quickly made for the bridge, with more heading for the engine room. *Lavish's* Captain watched though his binoculars as his men went around the ship. He noticed a muzzle flash on the enemy bridge, and a moment later they heard a report of a gun. His officer stood on the enemy bridge wing and waved — all OK. It was obvious that the ship was sinking, so the boarding party was ordered off. A short time later, as the launch bumped alongside *Lavish*, the officer in charge had a huge smile on his face and was eager to get to the bridge. He had a duffle bag in his hands that looked heavy, and around his neck was draped a Jap ensign and some binoculars, trophies!

Lieutenant John Sumner arrived breathless on *Lavish's* bridge. The Captain was waiting for him. "OK John, tell me what happened."

"Sir, we made our way to the bridge where we found a Jap naval officer stuffing these books, I guess they are code books, into this bag" He pointed to his prize. "He raised a pistol at me and the buffer shot him."

The Captain nodded. "Carry on."

"The engine room was found to be empty, but the sea cocks had been opened. There was nothing we could do down there. We had a quick look in the hold; all we could see was sacks of rice, and ammo for the Jap army."

The ship was the *Ling Sun no4*, a Malaysian ship, that had been taken over by the Japs. Clearly, they weren't happy with that arrangement, hence the flag in the 'oggin'.

"Sir, we have a steward onboard who worked on P & O; before the war he was based at Hong Kong. Should I ask him to have a look at the books?"

"Good idea, John."

The steward was summoned. He had a quick look. "Captain, I only know a little Japanese, but these are definitely Japanese naval publications. I don't know what they mean."

"Excellent, ask the Cox'n for an extra tot of rum." Turning away, he speaks again, "Bunts, tell the *Dido* what we have, light signal only — we don't know who's listening."

With that they headed back to the force at speed.

Later that day they met up with the rest of the force; *Lavish* closed *Stockport* to transfer the bag of code books. Before leaving Capetown, *Stockport* had taken onboard a party of Japanese cryptanalyst, so this was Christmas come true for them. While alongside, Lee stood at the bridge wing with the megaphone in his hands, saying, "Well done *Lavish*," which brought a huge cheer from the destroyer's crew.

As the small support fleet hove into sight. "CPO order the destroyers to refuel first then *Dido* and *Bellona*." After refuelling they cruised down the west side of the Andaman Islands. *Georgic's* aircraft again out a maximum range, searching for the enemy.

The following day, one of the aircraft spotted a small convoy hugging the east coast of the Andaman Islands. Lee ordered his ships to increase speed and head south; he wanted to catch the convoy as it passed a gap in the island chain. The spotter aircraft was kept on station, but a maximum visible range, so as not to warn the enemy. As he closed the convoy, Lee planned his attack.

Using *Stockport* and *Kent*, to bombard the convoy with gunfire, he would detach *Bellona*, *Lookout* and *Lively* to enter the gap between the islands and finish off the enemy. Another two Avenger was launched to act as gunfire spotting aircraft, and four fighters as escorts. The range was dropping rapidly, ships were at action stations, crews in anti-flash gear; sweating in the heat. "CPO Carrie tell *Bellona*, *Lookout* and *Lively* to detach and follow instructions."

Stockport and *Kent* would be indirect firing, over the top of a small hill on the island, they could not see the enemy. "DCT... Bridge range 10,000 yards, sir, permission to open fire."

Lee looked around the bridge, satisfied with what he saw. "Pass the word to *Kent*, Open Fire, go ahead guns."

The tannoy squawked, "Commence, commence," the last word unheard as the triple six-in guns on "B" turret, belched fire and smoke, and the clouds of cordite flooded the bridge.

Closed up in 'A' gun turret, De Asha could not see his target, but had to set his sights on instructions from the DCT, so providing they were right, all should be well. He looked across at Jenkins, who was shaking as he stood by the fuse setting instrument, and winked at him. The fire gong sounded near De Asha's head, ting, the confined space echoed around them with a terrific bang, and the stench of cordite filled the air. Nipper sat under the gun captains' stool and barked!

"*Ascot 1* to Father, down 100." Lee could hear the spotter aircraft calling in the ranging shots; *Ascot 1* was talking to his gunnery officer. "Shoot." The ting ting of the firing gongs sounded, as more shells was sent over the hill. Lee looked behind to watch *Kent's* shooting. "*Ascot* 1 down 50." Boom, silence. "*Ascot* 1 you have the range, fire." This time a full 12-gun salvo disappeared over the horizon. Followed by another three salvos. Moments later, "Target sinking, shift target, Red 025 up 200. Shoot!" Lee listened in to the conversation; it was going far better than he hoped. Salvo after salvo crashed out. "*Ascot* 1, target sinking shift target, Red 45 down 100 shoot." Another salvo of 6in shells went down range.

On the other side of the island, the small minesweeper *IJN Tenko*, and *Subhunter 23*, were cruising south, a small convoy of six coasters, following in a rough box shape. The weather was warm and sunny, with a gentle swell, the bridge party were relaxed and not keeping a good lookout, after all there were no enemies around here. In the distance, they could just make out an airplane, buzzing about; it was assumed that it was a friendly aircraft, and was soon forgotten. The Captain of *Tenko* was looking across at the nearest ship, when suddenly three water spouts rose from the sea. Looking up at the sky he searched for the aircraft that had attacked them. Again, three water spouts rose nearer to his ship! What is going on. Then his world exploded around him as his ship shuddered under the assault of 6in shells. Astern of the convoy *Subhunter 23* disappeared under the shells from *Kent*, then one by one each of the six merchant ships were taken under fire, again from an unseen enemy. Emerging from the gap in the islands, three warships were spotted, they quickly spread out and launched themselves at the defenceless merchantmen.

On the other side of the island *Stockport* and *Kent* ceased fire; it was *Bellona*, *Lively* and *Lookout's* turn. They soon fell on the cargo ships with a gusto, and after one hour there were eight piles of debris floating in the water, with men trashing about. The lone minesweeper, smoking badly and seriously damaged, was trying to carry out rescue operations. *Bellona* and the destroyers instructions were to return to the force, so the survivors were left to look after themselves. The ships formed into line ahead and headed back through the gap in the islands and returned in triumph to the rest of the force. On all three ships, they had a broom tied to the foremast. An ancient traditional sign, that said, for all to see, "that the enemy had been swept from the sea!". The force continued south, their first two engagements with the enemy over. OK they're no particular match for the force, but it was still a victory.

Talking on the TBS with *Georgic's* Captain, Lee explained his next actions, but stressed that he wanted to keep the presence of the carrier a secret, but there would be plenty action soon. While the Captain understood, his young, fire breathing SPLOT (Senior Pilot) wanted more action. Lee smiled. They continued south; their speed restricted to that of the auxiliaries. The compass showed a heading towards the Cocos islands. Their orders were to check them out — this was regarding some strange activity reported there. The sea was gentle, with a warm breeze, but the temperature was rising inside the ships, as the drew nearer to the equator.

Lee studied his ships one by one, they all appeared competent and well trained, a tribute to their Skippers, especially with so many Hostilities Only ratings onboard. Lee had stressed to his ships' Captains the importance of proper hydration and fresh fruit and vegetables; he did not want his crews coming down with prickly heat and scurvy, common in the tropics. Looking across towards *Empire Brecon,* he was happy that she was with him. Taken up from trade, she had been a 'Banana Boat', a refrigerated transport from the Montevideo to Liverpool run. Now painted in 'Pusser Grey' and fitted with anti-aircraft armament, her role had changed dramatically. Alongside her was the Naval Tanker *Blue Rover*, built for the Royal Navy, she also was well equipped to defend herself. Now fitted with new refuelling gear, copied from a captured German tanker, it was more adaptable and easier to use than the standard RN gear. Her skipper was 'top notch' and was happy to be under Lee's command.

Lee's gaze was interrupted by the bridge phone. "Sir, can you come down to the coding room?"

"On my way, you have the bridge, No 1."

Entering the tiny code room, one of the ratings left to give Lee some space. Dave Vickers, another survivor from *Preston's* sinking and now promoted to Sub-Lieutenant, was responsible for codes and cyphers. He spoke first, "Sir, the code books that *Lavish* recovered are the latest codes for the Jap fleet, they also list this month's planned movements for shipping in this area."

"Great, go on."

"That convoy we destroyed was going from Cox's Bazar to Port Blair then onto Banda Aceh, loaded with munitions and rice for the Jap Army."

"From what we have read, there is a small squadron of destroyers cruising this part of the Andaman Sea and the Malacca Straights.".

"Do we know where they are at the moment?" Lee asks.

"Sir, from our reading of this, we think they are off Penang."

Lee thought for a moment. "OK how many destroyers?"

"Sir, we can make out three call signs, but there may be four, sorry sir that's the best we can do." Vickers looked apologetic.

Lee smiled. "Don't worry, Sub, you and your team have worked wonders. OK this is what I want you to do — copy everything — I will contact 'their Lordships' and get a plane to us and we can forward the books on for the 'Intel' guys to look at." Lee thought for a moment, then asked the CPO in charge, "Can we monitor their signals traffic?"

The CPO nodded and smiled. "Yes sir, now we have the frequencies, we can track most in this area, but sir, I only have two Japanese speakers on board, we will be struggling to keep up. Can I have another radio operator to ease the load?"

Lee's mind was working overtime. "I have a better idea, Sub, clear that space in the passageway and close off the hatch, so there is only one entrance, get the Buffer to help, set up a plotting table, and track what ships you can on it. Sub, you are now in charge of the operation, report only to me. I will see if there are any other translators available, understood?"

"Yes sir," with nods all round.

"Well done all of you, well done," and with that Lee left for the bridge.

Returning to the bridge, Lee spoke to Chief Yeoman Carrie, and dictated a signal for the Admiralty to be sent urgent and top secret; he them sent a private message to all his ships' Captains asking them to check if he had any Japanese speakers on board, and finally he told Watson in confidence about what he was planning. Sat in his chair, enjoying a cup of coffee, "Plane approaching, sir, signalling 'enemy in sight',," at that moment the TBS squawked, "From *Georgic*, Japanese destroyer forty-five miles to the southwest heading southeast, *Minekazi* class." The report was electrifying, grabbing the TBS handset. "*Georgic*, this is *father*, was the aircraft spotted."

"He doesn't think so, the destroyer is on its own, nothing in the area," came the reply.

Jumping from his chair he heads for the chart table, where Backhouse the navigator was already plotting a course to intercept. "OK pilot, how long to intercept?"

"About three hours, sir."

"Thank you." Returning to his chair, "Bunt's contact, *Bellona*, *Lookout* and *Lively*, tell them to intercept and sink that destroyer." Picking up the handset again, "*Bellona* this is *father*, make sure you jam any signals from that ship, they must not get a message away, telling the enemy we are here."

"Understood."

Lee watched as the three ships leapt forward, smoke belching from their funnels, as if waiting for the signal, and headed off to the southwest.

A short time later, a voice next to him spoke, "Message, sir."

"Thanks Chief."

"Pilot set a course to the West southwest, we need to be at this location at 0800 tomorrow to meet up with a Sunderland flying boat, also ask Mr Vickers to come to the bridge."

"Aye, aye, sir."

"Message, sir."

"Thanks, Chief." Passing the message across to the Captain, it was from *Blue Rover*; they have a second officer onboard who can read and write Japanese, who served on the KKY lines before the war, *Lavish* has a steward who can speak a little, and *Kent* has a CPO who was born in Japan. "CPO send a signal, transfer these men to *Stockport* immediately, for short duration."

With the transfer of these men, Vickers was able to copy and translate all the code books, just in time to meet the Flying boat.

Yorktown continued her stately progress towards Bombay, now heading NNW across the Indian Ocean. The crew had settled down to their slow journey. The sky was deep blue and the Ocean a deeper blue. The crew were becoming very complacent.

To the south, Commander Dave Wilkinson, Captain of the Dido class light cruiser, *Bellona*, was watching the range to the Jap destroyer close slowly; it was just in range of his 5.25 in guns, but he wanted to be a little closer. He had ordered the two destroyers to move out to port and starboard so as not to mask each other's gunfire. "Captain, they spotted us," came a shout from the masthead lookout. Smoke and sparks issued from the funnels of the destroyer as she piled on speed and started to weave. "Sir, she's broadcasting."

"Jam her signals, open fire guns."

Ting Ting went the firing gong, Crack as "A, B and Q" turrets fired ranging shots. Tall water spouts rose around the fleeing destroyer, her battle ensign streaming from her yard arm — she could not retaliate her guns did not have the range. Ting Ting, another salvo landed next to the destroyer. Wilkinson ordered his destroyers to attack independently. "She's turning to Port, sir," came the cry.

Ting Ting and another salvo landed close to the enemy ship. She turned broadside to port and fired torpedoes at her tormentors, clearly visible from *Bellona's* bridge. The cry: "Torpedoes in the water."

This surprised Wilkinson, 'at this range' he thought 'no'.

Onboard *Yakaze*, Captain Jenko knew he could not out fight these enemy ships as he was alone and short of fuel. He had been heading back to Penang, after a patrol in the Indian Ocean, where he had shot down and captured some English Airmen. He was clearly outnumbered. He turned to fire his Type 93, 'Long Lance' torpedoes, the Japanese secret weapon. These were massive 'ship killers', 24in in diameter, fast, oxygen fuelled and a range of twenty miles plus. He was hoping to cripple or sink at least one of these enemy ships. The torpedoes were unknown to the Royal Navy; these were the first time they had encountered them. The ship shuddered; two heavy shells plunged though the stern of his ship. These were followed by a third which passed straight through the engine room and again out of the bottom of the ship. Standing on the bridge, his families Samurai sword impotent in his hand, Captain Jenko went down with his ship. Unknown by anybody, Birch, Smith and Bell had been avenged.

"Torpedoes dead ahead." Wilkinson leapt to the front of the bridge; there directly in front, two lethal looking torpedoes with shiny red warheads pasted either side of his command. "Where the hell did, they come from?" he asked the bridge in general.

"I have been trying to contact the bridge, sir. They came from that Jap destroyer, sir. I have watched them all the way," the foremast lookout called.

"Thanks, recall the ships, let's make way to rejoin."

As the little force turned and retraced its course. "Object in the water," called the starboard lookout.

Wilkinson looked over the bridge screen to study the object. "Guns?"

"Sir, it looks like a torpedo."

"You are right, Guns. No1, stop the ship, away a boats crew to recover it, Torpedo officer to assist." Giving anti-submarine protection, the two destroyers circled. *Bellona's* boats crew were struggling with this monster weapon. A lot bigger than the standard Royal Navy torpedo, it took considerable effort to hoist it aboard. When the Torpedo officer had disarmed it. He found that the nose fuse had jammed before or during launch, hence it hadn't exploded at the end of its 'run'. Being metric sizes, the Engine room machine shop had to adapt a few tools to fit. What a prize, the torpedo officer spent many happy hours dismantling it and taking notes! As they got closer to the rest of the Force 'Y', Wilkinson was able to talk to Lee, and briefly give him a rundown on the operation and the recovery of the torpedo.

Chapter 4

S*tockport* and the rest of the force were waiting for the arrival of the Sunderland. Lee did not like having his ships stopped in the middle of the Indian ocean, so had set a strong aircraft and destroyer antisubmarine shield around his ships. He also took advantage of a chance to refuel and resupply. The Sunderland was late, very late, and Lee was worried. Eventually it hove into view, smoke streaming from one of its engines; it circled and then commenced its landing run, fire now pouring from its two port engines. "Away launch and longboat, assist the aircrew," Lee ordered. The Sunderland landed, and made for the *Stockport*, where it commenced to sink. The crew scrambled out of the aircraft and were able to pass over to the launch some packets, mail, and Admiralty signals pouch, then the aircraft sank, leaving a small pool of petrol afire on the surface.

A very wet and bedraggled Flight Lieutenant arrived on the bridge, clutching the Admiralty pouch. Saluting Lee, he handed it over. Mr Vickers took possession of it and scampered of to his office to open it. A growing puddle of sea water gathered around the airman. "Sorry sir, we spotted a Trawler that didn't look right; when we went to have look it opened fire on us."

"OK Lieutenant, get yourself off and get dry. Messenger, take the officer and crew to the wardroom and ask the steward to look after them."

They had to await another day for a replacement Sunderland to arrive. Which worked out OK in the end, as *Bellona* was able to also pass over the drawings and photographs that they had taken of the enemy torpedo. After the replacement Sunderland had departed, with its precious cargo of code books, torpedo drawings and a very happy spare Sunderland crew, and including Lee's dispatches for the Admiralty. "OK Pilot, set a course for the Cocos Islands, speed 18 knots."

Onboard *Georgic*, a Wildcat fighter was landing; it missed the arresting wire and crashed into two other Wildcat fighters writing them off. Lee thought if we carry on like this, we will have no aircraft for the enemy. Mr Vickers came onto the bridge and spoke quietly in Lee's ear, "Sir, we have just decoded a message that's a few days old. It's from the destroyer *Yakaze* to Penang, reporting the capture and execution of two British Airmen, and it gives our missing airmen's names!"

"Very good, keep it to yourself for now. I will contact *Georgic*."

"Sir, also that was the name of the destroyer that *Bellona* sank."

"Thanks." A burning anger grew inside Alan's body at this news; he said a silent prayer for them both. They continued south. As they passed Great Nicobar Island, Lee ordered *Lavish*, *Lightning* and *Dido* to make a sweep down the west coast of the island, to see if any shipping was around. Lee watched as they increased speed and turned East.

It was a sad conversation with Pat Byrne, the skipper of *Georgic* and his Senior Pilot, Dave Johnson, the SPLOT, about the fate of the airmen. He got the feeling that that the retribution from the aircrews was going to be severe. Next day they continued south. Their strike force returned to Force 'Y' with nothing to show for its excursion. The sea remained benign, and smooth with a very gentle swell. Lee watched as another search aircraft was launched to keep them safe. Later four Wildcats were launched to practice interceptions and shipping strikes, using *Empire Brecon* as a target. Later that day *Brecon* must have got fed up with being a target and signalled to the fighters "To bugger off and practice on somebody else". This made *Stockport's* bridge crew chuckle.

Andy Watson kept the crew busy, drills, exercises and painting ship. Lee was happy the way the crew were getting better and more efficient. Still, they headed south. The following day after the morning search had been launched to give his crew a 'make and mend' period. This allowed the off-duty watch to relax for a few hours, later followed by the on-duty watch. This clearly went down well with his crew. Lee left the bridge, and went to his day cabin. He knew that paperwork was waiting and he had been putting it off. With a sigh he got stuck in to it.

Much later as the sun was going down, his steward Bob Pardoe came into close the deadlight. "Would you like something to eat, Captain?" He realized he was starving.

After eating he studded the Admiralty chart of the East Indies, and was trying to formulate a plan. He woke up hours later, with a very stiff neck and a bruise on his forehead, where he had hit his desk when he fell asleep! Annoyed he got up, grabbed his cap and went for a stroll around his command.

As another beautiful day dawned, it found Lee sat in his bridge chair. The visibility was excellent, and again a warm breeze caressed the bridge. Gentle conversations were going on around the bridge by the duty watch. The bridge messenger approached him. "Sir, a message from Mr Vickers: could you go to the coding office please?"

"Thank you, very well, Pilot, you have the bridge." Lee had made the decision to put a Marine Guard on duty at the entrance to the cabin; he did want to keep all this a secret. The marine saluted and opened the door for him. "Thanks, Marine Bennett," as he entered and closed the door. "Now Mr Vickers, what have you got for me?"

"Oh, sir, we have a lot. We have worked out that there are three destroyers based at Penang, all of the *Minekazi* class of second-class destroyers. Penang launched a 'Emily' class flying boat to search for that destroyer we sank but found no evidence so have called off the search."

"Good," whispered Lee.

"From what we can work out, there are two heavy cruisers, *Tone* and *Takao*, three light cruisers *Kiso*, *Tama*, and *Oi*, and seven destroyers of destroyer Squadron 17, all *Kagero* class (Big powerful ships armed with 5in guns), plus light forces, based in Singapore. We think that there is a carrier there also but we can't confirm it, but we thought you should know, sir."

Lee spoke, "Thanks, always tell me the worst-case scenario please."

"Will do, sir, also we have been monitoring Japanese radio communications to the south of us, sir. I don't know where we are heading, but at a guess, the lads think it's a fixed station."

"OK, that's great reporting. We are heading for the Cocos islands — do you think that signal is coming from there?"

"It could well be, sir. Its growing in strength, as we head south," replied the CPO.

"Right, do you have the frequency they are transmitting on?"

"Yes sir."

"Good keep it handy, I will need it later on. Bloody good work, keep it up." Lee left the cabin and headed back to the bridge, deep in thought. "Pilot, ask No 1 to join us in the chart room please." Lee had a plan.

The Cocos Islands, also known as the Keeling Islands, was a desolate lagoon in the Indian Ocean. Its only inhabitants were Frigate Birds, and a few employees from the British company Cable and Wireless — their job was to relay messages between Australia and Singapore and India. In late 1941 the Australian cruiser, *Sydney* had met the German Raider *Kormorant*, nearby. In the ensuing action both ships had been sunk, but no trace of *Sydney* or her crew had ever been found. A few German survivors had landed on the islands and had been taken away by the Australian navy.

Two days later, they were at extreme range for an Avenger aircraft to check out the Cocos islands; so with extra fuel tanks fitted, two Avengers were launched for their long trip south and back. In the meantime, Lee's coding team had been monitoring the signals from the islands, as they went further south the signals were getting stronger. Lee had insisted on total radio silence from the search aircraft, so it was six hours later that they reappeared on the horizon. Lee watched as they landed back on *Georgic*. Though his binoculars, he could see one of the pilots being helped out of the aircraft, stiff, the legacy of being too long at the controls. When they were able too, they reported on what they had found.

Firstly, there was a small freighter anchored in the lagoon, with a few smaller vessels travelling between it and the shore, the Cable and Wireless aerials, were still in use, and what looked like an airstrip being constructed on West Island, also some strange debris on the beach at Pulo Cheplo on eastern island. They also reported a Japanese flag flying over the Radio relay station. So now he had the information about the islands he could put his plan into action. Thus, began some furious activity between the various ships in the Force.

The Royal Marine detachments onboard *Stockport, Kent, Georgic, Bellona* and *Dido* were transferred to *Wren, Magpie* and *Lookout*, with a few men on *Lively*. This was going to be a traditional "cutting out operation" — something that the Royal Navy hadn't done for many years. *Lavish, Lightning* would provide Anti-submarine protection and *Dido* would close the islands for gunfire support, although Lee didn't think it would be needed, and Wildcat fighters would patrol overhead, to give any other support.

The dawn broke, with dark clouds in the sky, but the sea was calm. Royal Marines, armed to the teeth, with Lee Enfield rifles, Lanchester machine guns, grenades and cutlasses, some of them clambered down into the ship's boats, and set of in different directions. As the ships started their approach, *Stockport* and *Kent* proceeded to jam the radio frequency to eliminate any chance of the Island getting a signal away to warn the Japs. *Lively* went alongside the Freighter in the lagoon, *Wren* bumped into the jetty at the Radio Relay Station, *Magpie* and *Lookout* berthed on the jetty near the airfield. *Dido* cruised outside the lagoon entrance. The crew of the Freighter surrendered quickly. They were Javan's; it was not their fight, but they had Japanese officers, who were promptly shut in a cabin on the freighter. *Wren's* marines came ashore under fire, but a launch from *Stockport*, full of marines and sailors, led by the newly promoted Corporal Bennett, landed behind the Radio station, and were able to sneak up on a few soldiers holed up in a small bunker. Bennett ordered two grenades to be thrown at the bunker. The grenades did their job; three Japanese soldiers died. Across the lagoon, another small firefight was taking place, as Japanese soldiers tried to defend the airfield. *Magpie* and *Lookouts* Royal Marines stormed ashore, and after thirty minutes fighting, and two shells from *Dido*, the enemy were eliminated. Once the firing stopped, the marines were besieged by slave labourers from Korea and China, who were happy to see the marines, and the death of the hated Japs.

Lee ordered all the ships to berth in the lagoon. This would give his crews chance to stretch their legs, and some vital servicing could be carried out on the ships. Also four Wildcats were landed ashore to operate from the newly completed runway. The slave labourers had finishing it of in record time. A small party of 'Cable and Wireless' employees were found in a dark shed, where they had been starved and maltreated for weeks, and with their help, the radio was repaired. The food supplies found on the islands was distributed to the hungry slaves, and Lee organized supplies from *Empire Brecon* to be offloaded. The freshwater tanks were refilled from *Blue Rover*. Lee sent Corporal Bennett and a party of sailors and marines to inspect the strange debris off the beach at Pulo Cheplo. They discovered the remains of a ships boat, a scorched lifebelt with *Sydney's* name on it, various bits of timber and a metal cabinet, that contained files on the ships company. A message was sent to the Australian Navy at Darwen, explaining the situation, and they had promised to dispatch a supply ship and a couple of Aussie warships to regarrison the islands. Repairs finished, the crews rested, a small garrison of Royal Marines, under the command of a Sargent, were left to guard the remaining Japs, the aircraft recovered, Force 'Y' sailed for the Dutch East Indies.

As they neared Christmas Island, Lee detached *Bellona*, *Lively* and *Lookout* to circle the isolated island and report. They soon headed back to the force as all that was observed was a native village and a few small fishing canoes, so they withdrew and left them alone.

Intelligence had reported that small Japanese convoys were passing thought the Seribu islands and Krakatau gap then east along the coast. Lee was hoping to catch one of these convoys. One of the patrolling Avengers spotted what he had been looking for — a convoy of about twelve coasters and inter island traders, supported be two minesweeper and two sub hunters. They were heading for the Cilacap Bay. After speaking to Byrne and his SPLOT, the decided that 'The Fly Boys' could have first chance of attacking the convoy. He would then follow up with his cruisers.

Georgic launched a full strike of fourteen Avengers and six Wildcats against the convoy, with six Wildcats held as a Combat Air Patrol to cover his force. Once launched, he ordered the carrier, supply ships and their escorts to head south, away from danger. The Avengers fell on the convoy with glee, the first time they had been let of the leash. Armed with 500lb bombs and torpedoes it was a target rich environment. The Wildcats took it in turn to make strafing runs on the escort ships, as the Avengers attacked the freighters. There was no enemy air force to distract them. Once the Avengers were out of weapons, they returned to the carrier, where they were quickly reloaded and launched again. Soon the sea was littered with burning and sinking ships, their death palls rising high up to the sky. The strike force was ordered back to the carrier, after using up their weapons. With *Lavish* in the lead, *Bellona* next, the ships formed into line astern, and sped along the line of sinking ships. Opening fire, they finished off what the aircraft had started. As the sun was setting, there was nothing left to shoot at so they turned south.

Lee received orders from the Admiralty to head for Darwin Australia, at best possible speed. The US Navy wanted to look at that torpedo that *Bellona* had captured, as soon as possible. So, it was a happy band of sailors that headed southeast for Darwin. Giving the Dutch East Indies a wide berth they headed into the Timor Sea. Lee insisted on a CAP of fighters overhead at all times; being near the enemy airfields, he wanted insurance.

It was two o'clock in the morning, a pitch-black night. An almighty bang was heard and felt through the ship. *Yorktown* shuddered and began to slow down. The ship's siren began its ear shattering howl, as the gunners rushed to their gun, the ship's crew checked for damage and started to clear away the lifeboats. Soon the chaos onboard subsided, as the crew assess the damage. They had been torpedoed in number two hold, just in front of the bridge. A hole the size of a double decker bus in the ship's side, sheep carcasses and bags of rice could be seen floating out. As dawn broke, it was obvious that, although the ship was lower in the water, it was not sinking, in fact as the bosun and his men checked the holds there was very little water onboard. As the sun began to show, the lookouts spotted a submarine lying on the surface some distance away. From the markings on the control tower, it was a large Japanese submarine.

George Butler looked through his gunsight; this was the opportunity they had been training for, for the past two years, an enemy submarine, just in range. He ordered his gunners to lie on the deck, so the enemy would think the gun was un-manned. They watched, as the submarine started to circle *Yorktown*, as if the Captain was trying to figure what to do next! After a full circle, it started to move closer. The jap sailors started to man the deck guns, they had obviously decided to close the range and finish off *Yorktown* with gunfire. The submarine fired a ranging shot from one of its main deck guns. It fell well short. Butler watched as the sub came closer. The *Yorktown's* skipper was screaming from the bridge to open fire. Butler just waved his hand in reply.

With no return gunfire, the submarine became bolder and closed the range. At eight thousand yards, Butler ordered his crew to their feet. The sight was on. The first round slammed into the breach and Butler pressed the firing pedal. Nothing happened, it was a dud round! Quickly the crew took out the faulty round, which was tossed overboard. The next slammed into the breech — this one worked. The shell landed past the submarine, so sights were set down, and another round went on its way. Straddle. The gun fired again, the four-inch shell hit the tough hull of the submarine and ricocheted into the sea, but they had the range. The sub fired it two main guns; both hit *Yorktown* forward, passing through the wafer-thin steel of the old steamer. *Yorktown* gun missed with the next two rounds, but the seventh one went straight though the conning tower leaving a huge cloud of sparks. The crew started cheering. The next Japanese shell hit the poop, just below where they were all standing, a terrific flash and bang and shrapnel scythed across the deck, hitting many of the crew.

Butler woke up lying on the deck. His ears were ringing, and he became aware of his men lying around him in unnatural possess. Pulling himself back to the firing seat, he aimed again at the sub. This shell hit and pierced the hull, and moments later smoke and flames could be seen. Some of the gun crew got back to their feet, as Butler screamed at them to reload. Firing again, they missed — fatigue was now catching up with them. Another shell landed in the sea abreast the forward sub gun. The shrapnel wiped out the Japanese gunners. Butler had blood running down his face as he tried to clear his eyes, as his next two rounds missed. Then they made another hit on the submarine hull aft, which left a huge scar in the steel. The

Japanese Submarine Captain had had enough; he turned North and headed away into a rain squall to lick his wounds. The surviving crew on *Yorktown* began tending to the wounded, repairing the damage, and getting the engine started. Four hours later, the boiler room had raised enough steam to get underway. Bulkheads were shored up, and the wounded made as comfortable as possible. They continued NNW at five knots.

The following evening again at two in the morning, there was an almighty crack, and the ship lurched to port and stopped, and began to sink. Three of the four lifeboats had managed to get away with the surviving crew and the wounded. The bosun was in the same boat as Butler and he explained that the cargo of rice, being wet had expanded as it absorbed the water. It became so large that it actually split the ship into two pieces, which then sank. Fortunately, the Radio operator had managed to get out an SOS, which had been acknowledged by the port of Darwin.

The following day, the *HMIS Jumna* came across the three lifeboats. The sloop's crew took onboard the survivors, and with great care looked after the wounded. She then headed to Darwin. The following night, a submarine was spotted, diving, on the radar set onboard the Indian Sloop. Being short of fuel and time, *Jumna* made two depth charge runs on the submerged sub, then unable to check for a result, continued towards Darwin. In two thousand feet of water the Japanese submarine *I.67* imploded and sank to the cold dark ocean floor.

Chapter 5

There was a terrific tropical storm lashing across the anchorage at Darwin when they entered. The rain had such force that it was painful for the crews who were on the open decks. The *Blue Rover*, aided by two tugs, was berthed at the fuel farm, where her depleted tanks could be refilled. *Brecon* was assisted to the small naval pier, where her food stocks could also be replenished. Also, alongside another small pier, was an Indian Navy Sloop, *Jumna*, offloading survivors from a sunken ship.

A landing craft, flying the American flag, scurried out to meet *Bellona*. The Americans were eager to get their hands on the Japanese Torpedo. The rest of Force 'Y' berthed in the river, but being so close to the enemy, an anti-aircraft watch had to be manned, in case of a surprise attack. Lee was summoned ashore to meet the Australian Naval officer in command in Darwin.

Lee took with him copies of the code books he had acquired also notes and photos of the Jap Torpedo. In his mind it was all very good London and the Americans having the information, but the Australians should have it as well. Fortunately, his code team, and the Torpedo Officer on *Bellona* had made a few copies *'just in case!'*.

He was already wet through by the time he boarded his launch. When landed at the Naval Pier he was pleased to see a Naval staff car waiting to meet him. The Australian rating, tall and bronzed, was a very cheerful chap, who insisted on talking all the way to Admiralty House. On arrival was another tall, tanned Australian Lt Cdr, was waiting with his hand out to greet him, and ushered him inside out of the rain. Like all buildings in this part of Australia, it had a corrugated tin roof, and the rain drumming on it, making speech nearly impossible, but it was dry, if not humid.

Ushered in, to see the Rear Admiral, Lee sat and explained what had happened since they left Trincomalee. The Admiral was hanging on every word, his secretary taking masses of notes. Two hours later, they sat down to lunch; the Admiral and his aides were still asking questions about their trip down. During the lunch, there was a noise, and raised voices outside the door. It then opened and aggressive US Navy Commander stormed in, asking to speak to Lee. Before anybody could speak: "Are you the guy who captured that Jap Torpedo?" The American spoke, looking at Lee.

In a soft voice he replied, "It was one of my ships, that collected the Torpedo, a ship under my command."

"Well god damn it, why did you dismantle it? It is now US Navy property, and we want all documents that you have made on it." The man was furious.

Lee put down his cup of coffee and looked at the American Officer. The Rear Admiral started to stand, and Lee looked across and spoke, "Sir, I can deal with this!"

"Commander, whoever you are, you have not introduced yourself, but never mind, that Torpedo is property of His Majesty's Navy and as such it is being lent to the US Navy for examination. It will remain the property of the Royal Navy until our bosses decide otherwise."

The American was just about to cut in when Lee spoke again. "As for information, you have everything that has been written down on the subject." He didn't allude to the fact that there was a copy in this office, and another onboard *Stockport*. "Furthermore, my Torpedo Officer had to disarm it and remove the warhead *ON MY INSTRUCTIONS*. Now I have nothing more to say, so please leave the building."

Lee turned his back and commenced eating his lunch. The American, turned on his heel and left the room, slamming the door behind him and was heard muttering, "Damn Limey's."

The Rear Admiral spoke, "I am so sorry, Alan, that was out of order. I shall speak to Captain Morehouse later about this incident," he went on, "The Yanks treat us like second class citizens, a "fetch me, carry me," force, they think that they are in command here. I have to slap them down every so often, *BUT* they are generous, we want for nothing!" he added.

After lunch, they discussed Force 'Y's next operations. Lee asked about replacement aircraft, to replace the Avengers and the Wildcats lost on trip down. He was informed that there was a US Navy pool of spare aircraft at the airfield but didn't know how to acquire them. Lee made his goodbyes and returned to his ship, furious that the Australian Admiral had let the Americans treat him with so little respect.

Later, in his day cabin, he was going through the endless piles of paperwork when his telephone rang. "Sir, OOW here, there is an American workboat that wants to come along side; it has a four ring Captain onboard."

"OK, Guns, have a side party mustered and allow him to board. I am on my way up."

Moments later he was stood on the quarterdeck, and the side party was offering due respect to a Captain of another Navy. A small Honour guard of Royal Marines had arms presented. The USN Captain saluted the quarterdeck, and then Lee. He was followed by two other Lieutenants and the Lt. Cdr. from earlier in the day.

Lee stepped forward. "Welcome onboard *HMS Stockport*. I am Captain Alan Lee," and held his hand out. This was firmly shaken by the pleasant looking Captain.

"Thank you, sir. I am Captain Theodore Morehouse, base Commander here in Darwin; may I introduce my staff, Lieutenants, Paine, Briscoe, and Lt Cdr Lovett, who you met earlier — he has something to say to you."

A shame faced Lt Cdr stepped forward. "Sir, I am very sorry for the way I spoke to you earlier; it will never happen again. I am sorry."

Lee stepped forward and stuck out his hand. "That's OK, Commander, all is forgiven," but underneath he was seething.

Captain Morehouse spoke, "OK, Lovett, you may return to your post." He abruptly turned and left for the workboat and disappeared towards the shore.

Lee spoke again, "Guns, will you take these officers for a tour of the ship, and entertain them in the wardroom. Captain Morehouse and I will be in my Day cabin."

Lee led the way to the hatch down to his cabin. Out of earshot of everybody Captain Morehouse spoke, "May I call you Alan? I am sorry for Lovett's manners. He's from Texas, and manners are not their strong suit. He should not have behaved like that. I am sorry."

Lee nodded. He pointed to the settee and pored a glass of scotch whiskey for his guest, then followed a very pleasant few hours as the two Captains talked about past ships and ports, and Morehouse was eager to hear about Lee's war. Later as he was leaving, his two officers in attendance, a little bit worse for wear, Lee asked about any spare aircraft.

"Sure, just go to the airfield and Paine here will sort you out."

Lee escorted them to the gangway where *Stockport's* launch was waiting to take them back to the naval pier.

Next day, before lunch, Lee and Pat Byrne, along with Dave Johnson the SPLOT and a case of whiskey, landed on the navy pier and commandeered a RAN Jeep. They then headed for the airfield. When they arrived at the Guardhouse, an American Soldier just waved them through and pointed in the direction of the airfield offices. They soon found Paine, asking him if it was possible to have two Avengers and a Wildcat. Paine looked perplexed. "Gee, we only issue them in batches of six so no I can't give you one or two, but you can have six of each." On seeing the case of whiskey he added, "Do you want six more of each?"

This is how twelve brand new aircraft, in USN camouflage, and with hastily painted British markings, arrived onboard HMS *Georgic*! The rest of the force rested and carried out repairs, with the assistance of the small naval dockyard staff. Fortunately, these were minor repairs.

Chapter 6

A week later they set sail. Their orders were to proceed through the Timor Sea, enter the Savu Sea, circle around the Island of Timor and bombard the port of Dili, where some Freighters had been reported. As they proceeded northwest, yet another tropical storm suddenly fell on the Force. It lasted thirty mins, then disappeared; this left the ships with steaming decks as the fierce sun dried out the ships upperworks. Just before Force 'Y' left the Timor Sea, Lee ordered his supply ships and their escorts to a rendezvouses point south of Timor. He then increased speed and proceeded into the Savu Sea. Again, his Avenger aircraft out ahead looking for trouble. The bridge watch were relaxed, yet vigilante, when the radio repeater on the bridge burst into life: "Sunray to Mother, one large tanker, and two escorts heading east, range fifty-five miles, over." This had the desired effect of waking everybody up.

Before the Officer of the Watch could pick up the phone, Lee arrived on the bridge, making straight for the chart table. After studying it for a few moments, he called up *Georgic* on the TBS, "*Georgic*, this is Father, over."

"Ask the Senior pilot to organize a strike force for that tanker."

"Bunts, tell *Dido, Lively* and *Lightning* to proceed towards the enemy, and finish off anything the aircraft leave afloat."

Mr Vickers came on the bridge. Lee spotted him and beckoned him over. "Sir, the code books are no use now; we have moved into another Jap area. However, we are picking up multiple radio contacts. We will do what we can."

"Thanks, Mr Vickers."

Later, as Lee watched the strike force leave the carrier, he was debating his next course of action. So far things had gone well, and after the past few years, it was nice to be 'dishing it out' for once. He stood up and moved over to the Radar repeater to watch as his strike force moved further into the Savu Sea. He could see the tanker and escorts, *Dido* and the destroyers moving to intercept, but something caught his eye, just inside the maximum range of the radar — a small group of dots were heading south.

Picking up the TBS he was about to call *Georgic* when she called him. "Hello sir, one of the search aircraft has sighted enemy ships at extreme range entering the Savu Sea; from the Komodo straights, we are waiting for an update."

Commander Bob Peel, onboard *Dido*, was studying the aircraft as they attacked the enemy tanker. One of the escorting destroyers was stopped and down by the stern, with black smoke pouring from her, the other destroyer was weaving around the tanker trying to give some protection. The tanker was high out of the water and was clearly empty heading to one of the many oil refineries to fill up. It had been hit by three bombs already but showed no sign of sinking. With about 20,000 yards to go he ordered his ships into line a head with *Dido* leading.

The remaining Japanese destroyer suddenly realized the danger, and turned to face *Dido* and her consorts, leaving the tanker to her fate. As she steadied on her course, she was rocked by an explosion; one of the Avengers had launched a torpedo at the tanker, but by mischance the destroyer turned into its path. The torpedo hit the forward boiler rooms, which tore the ancient destroyer apart, and she sank quickly. A few moments later *Dido* opened fire on the now defenceless tanker. It did not last long.

Peel stood at the bridge screen, watching as the aircraft formed up and headed back to *Georgic*, when his communications CPO passed him a message. "From *Stockport,* sir." He read the message: 'Enemy ships to the Northwest, stay where you are, I want to catch them in a pincer movement and drive them towards you, await instructions, Lee out.' Well, he thought this could be an interesting day.

On the light cruiser, *Oi*, with her sister *Tama*, along with the destroyers *Urakaze* and *Arashi*, members of the DesRon 17. This should have been a simple escort mission, two fast tankers and a Naval auxiliary to go from Dili to Cebu in the Philippines. But the urgent calls from the second-class destroyer *Hasa* reporting being attacked by American aircraft in the Savu Sea. The force was about forty-five miles away, so they increased speed to investigate. Captain Hito ordered his lookouts to search for enemy planes.

To the south, Lee watched on the radar repeater as the enemy ships increase speed and head towards the scene of the action with *Dido*. He ordered *Georgic,* when all the aircraft have been recovered, to launch a full strike against this force, but for now he wanted one aircraft to shadow them and report back. He then ordered his force to the northwest — to come up behind the enemy.

Captain Hito looked through his binoculars and could make out a tall thin line of smoke, but with the heat, it was hazy. The Japanese optics were the finest in the world, but he still could not make out what the smoke was from.

Peel in *Dido* retired a bit more to the south, he wanted to stay just out of visible range.

On *Georgic*, it had taken nearly two hours to recover the initial strike aircraft, refuel and rearm them. Now they were ready, led by Dave Johnson the SPLOT, seventeen Avengers, and twelve Wildcats, launched and assembled, before heading towards the enemy. The extra aircraft, "*acquired*" in Darwin, had made a significant increase in their strike capacity.

Lee was still watching the Radar repeater and with the flow of information from the spotter aircraft, he was reasonably certain of his opponent. Two light cruiser, and two Kagero class destroyers: these must have come from Singapore, part of the force his code team had told him about. The two cruisers were formidable opponents. Their design concept was different than European navies; these were made to lead massed torpedo attacks, and were armed with thirty torpedo tubes, ten banks of three tubes. The destroyers were also armed with eight torpedo tubes, two banks of four. Now with the information about the 24inch 'Long Lance' torpedoes, Lee had to be very wary of getting too close. What he didn't know about was the Japanese navy had perfected the technique of reloading torpedoes while at sea, something the Royal Navy had not thought possible.

Captain Hito heard the shout, "Aircraft approaching from the south" at the same moment that his masthead lookout shouted, "Warship masts near the smoke, to the east." Hito ordered the ships into line abreast and increased speed. He watched as the Avengers split into two groups — one came down to sea level, these were clearly torpedo planes, and the others went high, they would be the bombers. Some fighters also came down to sea level, but a few remained high, giving protection.

The masthead lookout called again, "Three warships to the east."

Hito ordered his guns to fire when the aircraft came in range. The two destroyers had dual purpose guns, so could elevate high enough to engage the bombers. His low angle guns commenced firing on the torpedo planes. Hito looked intently at the warships came into view: two destroyers, that were clearly British, and a strange looking cruiser with five main gun mountings, three in front of the bridge structure, and two aft. As he studied the cruiser, he saw her open fire. *Dido's* first salvo was good. It straddled *Tama*. He ordered his force to turn to port and launch torpedoes. As he turned, the first Torpedo plane dropped its torpedo, followed by the second and third. The bombers now joined in; the first 4, 500 lb. bombs landed between *Oi* and *Arashi*. The rest followed suit. Wildcat fighters now struck his ships, flying low they commenced to strafe the Japanese warships, inflicting major casualties to the unprotected gun crews. The first torpedoes missed due to the turn to port, but the remaining torpedo bombers, readjusted their approach and continued the attack.

Dido's third, and four salvos' fell on *Tama*. Hit repeatedly by armour piercing shells, she rapidly slowed down and turned to starboard a floating wreck. On *Oi*, the torpedo officer had lined up the *Dido* as his target. The two destroyers aimed at their opposite numbers *Lively* and *Lightning*. Captain Hito held the torpedo flag aloft in his hand so the other ships could see. He then dropped it with a flourish, as thirty deadly torpedoes enter the water, and sped on their way.

The bridge lookout called, "Enemy ships to the southwest."

No sooner had the lookout spoken, when *Urakaze*, came apart as eight inch shells pummelled her. *Kent's* first radar guided salvo had been direct hits. Five Semi-Armoured Piercing shells tore the ship apart.

On the flagship, Lee had ordered *Bellona* and *Lavish* to stay with *Georgic*. *Kent* and *Stockport*, with *Lookout*, were to increase speed and engage the enemy. It had been a perfectly timed attack, the Japanese force caught between two forces and an airstrike hitting them at the same time. They would talk about this at the Admiralty war college for years. Lee smiled. *Stockport* had to check fire, as *Lookout* in her rush to get at the enemy had fouled *Stockport's* range. Once clear, *Stockport* commenced slow methodical fire on *Oi*, hitting her with his second, fifth, and sixth salvos. The torpedo planes had targeted *Arashi* and *Tama*; for the loss of one aircraft they were again hit, and *Arashi* slowly capsized. *Tama* disappeared in a huge explosion. *Kent* shifted target and with *Stockport* pounded the unlucky *Oi*. Still firing her stern gun mounts, she finally sank, taking Captain Hito down with her.

In a poorly executed manoeuvre, *Dido*, *Lively*, and *Lightning* turned to port. Just as the swarm of Long Lance torpedoes arrived, hit by three torpedoes, *Lightning* disintegrated. *Lively* was slow to turn so was able to avoid the deadly missiles. *Dido* took one torpedo in the bow, "A", and "B" gun housing disappeared and the remaining deck, sagged down over the shattered bow, she slewed round and stopped.

"Damn, damn, damn, that should not have happened," shouted Lee as he pounded his bridge chair. Things had been going so well, now this. "Bunts, ask *Lively* to look for survivors, also all Force 'Y' ships converge on Father. Ask *Dido* if she can steam?"

"And tell *Lookout* to see if there are any Jap survivors."

It took nearly two hours for the force to reassemble. *Georgic* recovered her aircraft, two Avengers and a Wildcat were missing, and a patrol of fighters were launched to watch over them. There were very few survivors from *Lightning*. *Dido* had shored up her forward bulkheads and could steam at twelve knots, but she fell of course constantly the weight of the damaged bow pulling her to starboard. *Lively* had to be ordered to act as a rudder, by passing a stern line and towing to port. That was the only way to keep her heading in the right direction. Lee ordered a return to Darwin; this was not what he wanted, however his trip into the Savu Sea had been a success.

Lookout arrived at the area of most Japanese survivors; when she slowed down, they dropped scrambling nets to assist, but only a handful took hold of them. Everybody else turned their back on *Lookout* and swam away. One officer actually drew a pistol and started firing on *Lookout*. Captain Colin Marsh felt no regret at leaving the scene and returning to the force, his five Jap survivors in the forward mess deck wrapped in blankets and being given cigarettes. On meeting the flagship, *Lookout* transferred the survivors for interrogation by *Stockport's* Japanese speakers. The force then made their way back to Darwin.

Once joined by the support ships, the oil hungry destroyers going alongside first to refuel. The remnants of *Dido's* damaged bow fell off during the night, so *Lively* was cast off, and *Dido* continued to steer herself, if not in a straight line, then in a rough direction for Darwin. As they left the area, radar was watching a few enemy aircraft flying a search patten over the Savu Sea, clearly looking for the sunken ships.

Captain Lee kept a strong fighter cover over his force, just in case.

Chapter 7

Three days later, they arrived back in Darwin and a small welcoming party was there to greet them. This including the Royal Marines he had left on the Keeling Islands. Tugs assisted *Blue Rover* to the refuelling jetty and *Dido* was warped against the navy pier so emergency repairs could be started. Waiting in the roadstead were two "M" class destroyers, *Meteor* and *Myngs*, identical to the "L"'s. Lee was happy to see them; after the loss of *Lightning*, he could use some more destroyers.

He went ashore to meet with the Australian Admiral to report on the past few days. The Admirals Flag lieutenant, and Captain Morehouse USN was also there. They discussed many things, and Morehouse was impressed with his handling of his force's. "Thank you, Captain Lee, you did very well. I want you to take your force into the Banda Sea and sweep up to near the port of Ambon just of Maluku Island. There is an airstrip there called, Bandara Pattimura. We want you to attack it!" said Morehouse.

Lee looked questioningly at the Australian Admiral; his specific orders were not to do the bidding off the US Navy. "It's OK, Alan, I want this. There is some long range 'Betty' bombers there that have been attacking our coastal shipping, we want destroyed."

A few days later, *Dido* was towed out of the roadstead by an Ocean-going Salvage tug and escorted by two anti-submarine trawlers and a Patrol Sloop, began her long tow to Sydney to begin her repairs. As she departed, she was given a rousing cheer by the rest of Force 'Y'. Replenished and ready, The Force, plus the two new destroyers, departed a few hours later. Following the same formula, *Georgic* had her search planes out. The supply force was tucked in close, and the destroyers spread out in an anti-submarine screen.

Once again, the sea was crystal clear, visibility was unlimited, with a gentle swell, and warm winds. Lee stood up and left the bridge. "You have the ship, Pilot," and headed for the code and plotting room. The Royal Marine sentry, presented arm's, "Morning sir!"

Lee returned the salute. "Thank you, Marine Bennet!" Entering this cabin, he was hit by the heat. It was stifling. "We must see about rigging up some kind of ventilation for you," he said to the small number of ratings in there. "Mr Vickers, speak with the buffer, see what can be done."

"Right, what have we got?"

"Sir, we have been able to gather some more intelligence from the Americans. With the code books we captured, we have a rough idea of what is happening. The Japs changed their codes the other day so we are playing catch up."

"Go on."

"We know that our attack on the convoy has been reported, and the Japs have ordered a major sweep of the Savu Sea to locate us, they are under the impression it was the Americans. Also, two more cruisers and DesRon 12 have been ordered to Singapore — we don't have any names yet, with the codes changing."

"OK go on."

"We have tracked a couple of minesweepers and a second-class destroyer in the Banda Sea, but there is a signal we cannot decipher, we are working on it." To the cabin in general, "Well done everyone, you are making our jobs a lot easier thank you all, and Mr Vickers when you work out what that signal is, let me know."

With that he returned to the bridge.

North then North by West they headed at eighteen knots. Lee was giving the two new destroyers training exercises, and practice at refuelling and taking supplies on at sea, they needed to be up to speed with the rest of the force. They passed the south of Timur and entered the Arafura Sea, still steaming north. Once clear of the Arafura Sea, the entered the Banda Sea. Lee ordered all ships to refuel, then when this was completed, *Blue Rover, Empire Brecon, Wr*en and *Magpie* left to make to the new meeting point to the east of their current position. He then increased speed and headed for Ambon. This time, Lee did not detach *Georgic*, but kept her in the force. He suspected that she would need some protection when they stirred up the hornet's nest at the airfield. Radar reported, two inter island coasters, spotted heading east, with a small gunboat as escort. Lee ordered them to be left alone and altered course. He did not want to alert the Japs where he was; besides he could catch them on the way out and sink them then. He did however send a coded message to *Magpie* and *Wren* to be on the lookout for them, just in case.

The following day, the sea began to rise and the wind strengthened. Lee ordered the force to turn into the wind and slow down, His intension was to attack at first light the following morning if the weather permitted. Soon all flying had to be suspended, as the carriers deck started to pitch and roll badly. The weather did not abate, and the strike had to be postponed the following two days, the weather was far too rough.

On the second day, a small schooner was spotted, and *Myngs* was dispatched to capture it. When to schooner hove to, *Myngs* launched a whaler, and the sailors took possession of the small craft. There were six half-starved natives onboard, who were also happy to be rescued from service of the Japanese navy. There was no radio onboard and it was again carrying beer, and rice for the Jap Army, so it was decided to sink it. The natives cheering when *Myngs* Oerlikon gunners opened fire. The schooner did not last long in this uneven battle.

The wind and seas had died down overnight, so a recon. flight was dispatched the following day. This was to inspect activity on the airfield and around the dock areas. It was timed to arrive just as the sun was setting; the pilot was instructed to be 'up' sun, so it was nearly invisible from the ground. The downside, was it would return to the ship in the dark when its mission was completed. By following the carriers homing signal, the aircraft arrived overhead in the pitch dark. Lee ordered the carrier, in an action not seen before in wartime, to switch on the ships landing lights to assist the landing. The recon. aircraft landed safely with its vital information. The briefing for the pilots was very detailed; there was sixteen Mitsubishi bombers, known as 'Betty' to the Allied forces, on the airfield, some 'Emily' flying boats were moored in the river, and worryingly twelve Zero fighters dispersed around the landing strip.

In the predawn glow, Captain Pat Byrne looked down from the bridge; he could just make out the activity on the flight deck, as the aircraft were readied for the strike. He made eye contact with his Senior Pilot, Dave Johnson, who was sat in the cockpit of his Wildcat fighter. Although he could not see it, he knew that this aircraft was resplendent with the name *Carole Anne*, the name of Johnson's wife and a Vargas pin-up on the forward fuselage. Johnson gave the pre-arranged signal, a thumbs up. Captain Byrne, turned to the invisible bridge crew, "No 1, bring '*Big* G' into the wind and commence launching aircraft."

The first aircraft was Johnson, who had the shortest run up of any aircraft, and as he staggered into air, he dropped below the level of the flight deck. Byrne held his breath, as the fighter emerged into view, clawing for airspeed and height. He relaxed and watched as twenty Avengers and ten Wildcats took off and circled the ship, then headed of in the direction of the enemy airfield. When the strike was launched, he ordered the six remaining fighters to be readied on deck; these were his Combat Air Patrol, for protection of Force 'Y'. Below, stored in the lower hold, were the remaining five Avengers, and six Wildcats. They were parked as tightly as possible, with two hanging from the Deckhead, and while it was good to have additional aircraft onboard. Unfortunately, he did not have enough pilots to man them.

Dave Johnson, sat in his cockpit, looking down at the carrier as she launched the rest of the aircraft, kept making lazy turns, to Port, until all the aircraft had joined up on him. His engine set at a lean mixture and low revs, he needed to save fuel. As he watched the navigation lights and the exhaust glow race down the deck, once airborne the lights were turned off and they climbed up to join him. He kept his nav. lights on so they could see him; they would be turned off later.

He thought back over the past few years. He had entered the Royal Navy in 1938 and transferred to the Fleet Air Arm shortly after joining. He had read all the stories of daring do, from the pilots in the First World War, and that had excited him. After passing out, and gaining his wings, he was streamed into the Fighter Force; this suited him as he did not fancy the front-line strike aircraft of the day the Swordfish, "the stringbag". He was ordered to Lee on Solent to begin training on the latest Naval Fighter, the Blackburn Skua, a Dive Bomber / Fighter. He was not impressed. It was neither a good fighter or a good dive-bomber, but it was what they had been given. Later came the Blackburn Roc, a Skua with a turret behind the pilot, which housed four 303in machine guns. After the similar Boulton Paul Defiant had been decimated during the Battle of Britain, the navy wisely, removed them from front line service, but kept the Skua, until something better was available.

During his time on *Illustrious* he flew the Fairy Fulmar, again a two-seat fighter, with eight machine guns and a Rolls Royce Merlin engine, it should have been a great fighter, but it wasn't. It was heavy and slow and could not catch the bombers it was sent to intercept, and with no rear gunner it was vulnerable to astern attacks. It got so bad that a lot of the time, they flew without the observer, to lighten the aircraft. When they did have an observer on board, they took to taking a "Tommy gun" with them. Also, toilet paper was standard on most flights in enemy areas. Not for its intended use, but to throw in the slip stream of the Fulmar when it was being attacked; this had the effect of scarring of enemy pilots, the downside was that toilet paper was in very short supply for the ship's crew!

After his adventures in the Mediterranean, he was posted home to Hatston, where he trained on the American supplied, Grumman Wildcat. This was a fighter, tubby, sturdy, fast, manoeuvrable, roomy cockpit and six .05in machine guns, which gave more "punch" than the then standard RAF/RN issue 303in browning's machine guns. Having been promoted to Senior Pilot of an escort carrier, he was itching to get involved. The mission, so far, they had done well, but the enemy would test them out soon.

Once assembled, he turned them in the direction of the enemy airfield. It had taken longer than planned to get everyone airborne and in position, so the sun was rising when they were about fifty miles out. He ordered the fighters to increase speed and drop down to sea level, their job was to strafe the Zeros, that were parked at the western end of the runway, if all went well, they were then to attack the 'Betty's' and the 'Emilie's' berthed in the river, but the Zeros were priority.

About twenty miles out they overflew a Japanese patrol boat; it commenced shouting on its radio for all to listen, that it had been flown over by American aircraft. If he had time Johnson would have turned the force back and sunk the Patrol Boat, but the time was against them. His heart sank, as they got near the airfield, he could see aircraft airborne, obviously the Japs had an early morning patrol up! Still too late now.

He jabbed the radio transmit button, "Robin 1 (his call sign) commence attack."

The ten Wildcats swept along the length of the runway, firing as they went. The Japanese gunners were on form this morning, they had already started firing. The two fighters on either side of the formation, concentrating on the Zeros parked in their revetments. Johnson lined up on a Zero that had commenced its take-off run, his fired a short burst, and the Zero turned to the left and burst into flames. They had been told the Zero would not take punishment, if true then his first victory was no fluke!

Looking in the rear-view mirror (an addition, that Johnson had insisted on being fitted, to all the aircraft onboard), he could see flames and smoke on either side of the runway in his wake. He added boost and clawed for the sky, all the time straining his neck to look for any attacker trying to get behind him. To his right and slightly behind he spotted 'Woody' his wingman hanging on.

Another Zero passed from left to right, so he hauled on the stick to drop down on to it. He felt the Wildcat's frame groan as he piled on the 'G-forces' to get behind the fast disappearing Zero. The Zero made a mistake and turned right; this allowed Johnson to close the range. He looked through the red glow of his gunsight, a perfect deflection shot was on, he pressed the 'tit' and watched as a short burst of .50in bullets tore off the wing of the Zero. It turned on its back and spun down to the ground.

Climbing for altitude, he became aware of the radio chatter in his headset. As he turned to head back to the airfield, he watched as the bombers dropped their load of deadly eggs across the dispersal area. With explosions, smoke and debris flying into the air. He watched in horror as sporadic gunfire hit one of the Avengers, and it tried desperately to make its way out to sea, a natural reaction for all naval aviators — the sea means safety. Another Zero dived down and fired a long burst into the stricken plane. This also turned on its back and crashed in a fiery blaze across the runway. The Zero zoomed up and away, happy with his kill. One of his fighter pilots, who was closer than Johnson, raced after the Zero, its end coming very soon.

Johnson now had time to make sense of the attack, as he circled above the airfield. The six Zeros that were airborne had been shot down, the dispersal, where the rest of the Zeroes were parked, were littered with smoking wrecks. All the 'Betty' bombers were burning, large craters spread across the runway and the perimeter tracks. Out in the river, he could see six funeral pyres as the 'Emilie's' had all been hit and were sinking or sunk. He ordered the remaining Avengers to form up and head back to the ship. He led the fighters on a final strafe of the dock area, where they managed to set fire to the oil storage tanks. As they climbed away, he felt elated. The shaking would start soon as the adrenalin wore off. They had lost two Avengers and two Wildcats. He prayed they had a quick death; he hated the thought of his crews being prisoners of the Japs. The fighters closed on the bombers, and they all headed home to *'Big G'*, he spotted one Avenger limping along, its engine smoking. As he closed, he noticed the gunner in his turret slumped over his guns, and the Observer standing up in the cockpit leaning over the pilot, who was obviously having problem. He elected to fly formation on it, able to give help and advice.

Onboard *Georgic*, the radar reported that the strike was returning. Captain Byrne turned his ship into the wind for the aircraft to land. Waiting firefighting and medical teams standing by in case they were needed. Then one by one they arrived, throttles back, and the pop pop sound as the big radial engines backfired. After taking the arrester wire, then taxing forward to be struck down into the hanger. The last two to land was a badly shot up Avenger, with its Mid- Shipman pilot, badly wounded, then Johnson landed last. He had so little fuel left his engine stopped as he started to taxi forward. Byrne ordered an increase in speed and altered course to catch up with rest of the force.

Unknown to everybody and missed by the tired radar operator on *Big G,* a solitary aircraft had followed the strike back to the carrier. Just visible the Betty's crew watched which direction the ships were heading, and frantically passed the information back to Ambon. Just in time, as the two aircraft on CAP spotted the bomber. They raced to intercept it, making a slashing attack, that killed the cockpit crew and sent the bomber into a slow smooth dive into the sea. Apart from a small oil slick, there was nothing to betray the passing of the aircraft.

The phone rang, and awoke Lee, who was trying the luxury of a few minutes' peace. "Captain… Radio, we have picked up a transmission to the north of us. We think we managed to jam it but we are not certain!"

"Very good, I will come up." He made his way to the coding/plot room. "OK sub, what have you got for me?" he asked.

Vickers looked up from his chart. "Hello sir, we picked up a signal about thirty minutes ago. It was to the north of us. We think we managed to jam it, but we were at extreme range, so not certain. Anyway, *Georgic's* CAP shot down a Betty, which we think was transmitting, however the part of the message we decoded, gave our position, speed and direction of travel, as well as the composition of the force. I am sorry sir, just thought you should know."

Lee sat for a moment, thinking. "Right then, thanks, Subby, I think a change of plan is in order." Again, "Well done all of you, excellent job, keep it up."

He left the office. He called No 1, Pilot and Guns to join him in the chart room. He had come up with a plan and needed to share it with his officers for their ideas.

Later, after talking to his Captains on the TBS, ordered a course change, the bombardment was cancelled, and they increased speed and headed for his support ships. *Georgic* was not a 'proper' warship, she was a converted Passenger Liner, and although she could maintain 22/23 knots most of the time, anything faster was out of the question. His warships could make 30+, so they didn't make as much progress as he would have liked, plus *Georgic* had to keep turning into the wind to launch and recover aircraft. As good as the deck crew were, they still took longer than he had wished. Once again, he had the aircraft out at maximum range looking for the enemy. They soon found them, the small convoy they passed a few days ago, two small coasters and an old, captured gunboat. He would have liked to launch a strike, but he was aware that his flight crews were tired.

So, he ordered *Bellona, Meteor* and *Myngs* to close and sink them. The rest of the force continued towards the support ships. Two of the enemy ships were soon dispatched, the gunboat and one of the coasters sank with little fuss. On the second coaster, again the crew saw the British ships bearing down on them, and promptly launched a lifeboat, and everybody scrambled onboard, leaving the ship to sail on unmanned.

Dave Wilkinson on *Bellona* ordered *Meteor* to board the vessel and see if there was anything worth salvaging. This didn't take long, as they searched the ship it was obvious why the crew abandoned it. The forward hold was loaded with twenty 'Long Lance' torpedoes, and the aft hold was packed with, 5in, 6in and 8in shells, a floating bomb. Wilkinson ordered a scratch boarding party, with Stokers, Engine Room staff and a few seamen to head the ship towards a rendezvous with the support force. It soon became obvious that the best this ship could manage was eight knots, the report from the Engineers was, it was "clapped out" and no maintenance had been carried out in many years, due to cheapskate owners.

Once the hungry destroyers had been topped up with fuel, he ordered *Lavish* and *Lookout* to replace *Bellona* and the destroyers, also to refuel. Lee was starting to worry about *Bellona*; its fuel consumption was quite high, and along with the destroyers it needed topping on a regular basis. He thought about the message he received from *Bellona*, more of the large Japanese naval torpedoes onboard the coaster, much as he would have liked to take the Coaster as a prize, it was very slow and would become a liability. Therefore, he ordered it alongside *Brecon*, and ordered four torpedoes to be transferred, then anything of value, and sink it. They also found charts and notebooks, things of low-grade intelligence.

When all this had been accomplished, he ordered his support ships to leave the Banda Sea, and await him in the Arufa Sea. He then took his force east through the straights between Palau Tutun and Maluku and organized an airstrike on the airfield at Maluku Tenggara. He decided to follow the same procedure as the last strike, with a recon flight that night and a strike the following morning. It had been very successful last time, so there was no reason to think it would not work this time. However, things didn't go to plan. The recon. Avenger had engine problems, so was late taking off, thus it arrived late over the airfield. It was now so dark, very little could be seen, however it did wake up the anti-aircraft batteries, who lit the sky up, with tracer bullets and exploding shells.

Onboard *Georgic*, Johnson and Byrne decided that in view of the lack of intelligence that the strike force, would be eighteen Avengers loaded with 500lb high explosive bombs, and eight Wildcats to ground strafe. Which left only four Wildcats to guard the fleet. When told about this, Lee wasn't happy, but went along with the plan. This time the plan worked; they arrived over the airfield as dawn was breaking, nothing was flying apart from the strike force. Johnson tore across the airfield at low level, strafing anything that looked like an aircraft. As his fighters cleared the runway the bombers started their bomb run, this time with no opposition their bombs landed smack in the middle of the runway and among the aircraft hangers and workshops on the far side. Unfortunately, the Japanese gunners were on the ball, and Johnson watched in horror as three Avengers and two Wildcats, went crashing into the surrounding area. He spotted a gun pit with a triple barrel weapon sticking out, so he screamed down, firing his machine guns. The gun went silent, but he felt and heard a double bang at the rear of his aircraft. He had been hit. Then another bang under his feet. A heady mix of smoke, fuel and oil started to fill his cockpit. He headed out to sea, but his plane was not handling very well. It did not want to turn right, and it took all his strength to keep the nose up, the plane was hurting. He was aware of another aircraft next to him; it was Woody, his faithful wingman. His radio didn't work, so he followed Woody, as they headed out towards the carrier. The engine started to run rough, and it was clear he would not make it back. He just needed to get further away from the island.

Lieutenant Steve Wood looked across at his friend. Johnson's plane was badly damaged. He made the signal to say his radio was u/s. Steve acknowledged the signal. He was pained to see his friend and mentor struggling to stay in the air. Soon it was obvious that he could not stay airborne. The Wildcat getting lower and lower. The sea reached up and grabbed *Carole Anne*. The big radial engine did not make for a good seaborne landing, and the aircraft flipped on its back. Wood circled the crash site, praying for his friend to come to the surface. After ten minutes, there was no sign of Johnson, and his low fuel warning light started to blink, so he had to head back to the carrier, tears streaming down his face.

Lee watched the aircraft as they came back in ones and twos, as he watched it was obvious that they been badly shot up by the enemy. He counted only fifteen Avengers and five Wildcats return to *Georgic*. Clearly, there had been some enemy opposition. Once everybody was back onboard, they increased speed to clear the area as fast as they could, and he reflect on the action. Later, when he was talking to Pat Byrne, it was obvious that his aircrew were in a state of shock. The aircraft were starting to have faults and problems; three Avengers and a Wildcat would have to be stricken, as the damage was too great. Fortunately, the "replacement" aircraft would make up the losses, but it was the same problem, the shortage of pilots. The following day they met up with his supply ships, but this time, they headed east — their destination was Sydney.

Chapter 8

They crossed the Gulf of Carpentaria, hugging the coast of Northern Australia, through the narrow passage between New Guinee and Australia, every gun manned, and every fighter aircraft on alert — this was close to enemy territory. Hugging the coast, they continued down through the Coral Sea. They passed Cape Melville, Cairns and Townsville. Still, Lee had the Avengers out on patrol, watching for any sign of the enemy.

They passed Brisbane and entered the Tasman Sea. Lee relaxed the air patrols; they now had ariel protection from RAAF fighters, who set up a constant aerial cover, he could now stand his fighter pilots down from cockpit alert. About a hundred miles out, he met up with two Australian destroyers that had been sent out to escort them into Sydney. *Georgic* then launched all her serviceable aircraft to the Naval Yard at Nowra; they all need repairs and updates. The unserviceable ones would be craned onto a lighter in the dockyard and ferried ashore. It was strange to see her in the midst of his force with no aircraft on board. As they approached the Sydney Harbour Heads, and passed the boom, a small fleet of pleasure craft came out to meet them, and Lee became aware that crowds were gathering on all the vantage points and cheering in his ships. Once inside the safety of the harbour, *Stockport*, *Kent* and *Georgic* were directed to berth at Garden Island, *Bellona* and the destroyers had to pass under the famous Sydney harbour Bridge and berth at the Naval Dockyard at Cockatoo Island, *Blue Rover* at the fuel farm, and the *Empire Brecon* and the Sloops at various berths around the docks.

After his ships had tied up, the official meeting took place, a host of Naval Staff Cars, lined up at *Stockport's* gangway, and disgorged a whole line up of Admirals, Rear Admirals and Captains, who all trouped onboard for a hastily arranged meeting. Later after the visitors had left, Lee was stood on the quarter deck, as the men paraded for the first leave since Capetown, a long time ago. The Cox'n issuing the usual warnings about looking after themselves and VD. Lee was astonished to see a long line of cars all waiting to take his crews away for a few hours R & R. What wonderful people.

As peace descended on his ship, he was able to take a tour around his command, and speak to as many as he could, and thank them for their efforts. Over the next few days, he managed to make the time to visit every ship in his command, even making the trip to the Naval Air Station at Nowra to speak to his airmen. All these visits were well received. The whole force was in need of the dockyards help, so two weeks leave was granted to both watches, to allow the dockyards to commence the repairs.

De-Asha and Jenkins, and a few other mess mates made their way down the gangway, all dressed in their best white tropical suits, with clean HMS tallies on their caps. Coins sown into bell bottoms to make them swing better, immaculately pressed with the statuary seven creases. Shiny chrome watches on their wrists. At the jetty, De Asha, who had been before, led them towards the Fleet Canteen next to the Captain Cook Drydock.

After a couple of pints of beer he led them up 'Heart attack hill', the steep climb up to the 'Rock and Rover' pub, for some food. Jenkins was amazed; he had never seen food like this back home, and the quantities were huge! Now satiated they continued towards Kings Cross, to 'Harry's Pub', a well-known seaman's watering hole. Here they got into an argument with some Australian dockers; fists flew and the triumphant *Stockport's* men made a rapid exit. The few remaining mess mates made their way to the 'Taxi Club', another well-known sailor's pleasure palace. Here Jenkins became a man. Goaded on by De-Asa, he explored a willing woman for the first time. At five fifteen the next morning, the tired and penniless matelots made their way back onboard, just in time for curfew.

Lee was soon summoned to Admiralty House for a thorough debrief, so he took Watson, Vickers, Pat Byrne, Ray Arnold and Dick Rye from *Kent*. Dave Wilkinson would meet them there. This was going to be a long day for them all. With charts and deck logs, Lee went through all the actions from leaving Trinco' to the arrival at

Sydney. He explained his idea of setting up the plotting table and trying to read the Jap signals. He also expressed an opinion about having *Georgic* with him, while it was OK for now, any carrier for this operation needed to be bigger, faster and have more aircraft stowage, and more Fighters with spare crews. A Search and Rescue facility was needed to rescue downed pilots. He also complained about the "short legs" of *Bellona* and his destroyers. Ray Arnold, *Stockport's* Engineer, went into some depth as to the requirements and supplies needed for long term, long range operations, leaving a long and full list of his recommendations. Lee explained about sinking the coaster but taking four torpedoes for the Royal and Australian navies to begin to study them. He left a full and complete log of all his actions and recommendations for their Lordships to study.

It was after six in the evening before they were released, as they stood outside Admiralty House, waiting for their transport, Lee had an idea. "Well gents, that went well, dinner and drinks on me!" Just as their cars arrived, Lee spoke to the driver attached to *Stockport*, Garry Carne, "The Colonnades please, find us a good restaurant," as they all piled into the cars and headed for Glen St.

After midnight, and well inebriated, they left in the staff cars back to their respective ships. Carne and the other drivers making a pleasant journey back. The owners of the restaurant had flatly refused to except payment — truly wonderful people. Lee returned to the ship and slept the sleep of the dead.

Its Dec 1914. A very young and nervous midshipman stood at the quayside looking up at his new home. Towering over him was the latest of His Majesties warships. Resplendent in her gleaming dark grey paint of the British Grand Fleet. *HMS Caroline*, built at Cammell Lairds yard in Birkenhead on the Wirral, sat there dark and brooding. At four thousand five hundred tons, and a speed of 28 knots, she was the latest addition of one of the most successful cruiser designs for the Royal Navy. *Caroline* was ready to go to war. Alan Lee, Midshipman, had just got off the train at Portsmouth Harbour, and entering the dockyard, via the Main gate, showing his papers to the Sentry, he was allowed entrance to the busy, noisy dockyard. Walking down Main Rd, very conscious of his brand-new uniform, trying desperately to remain anonymous, he made his way to No 2 basin. Here was his home for the next two years. Having commissioned only a few days before, *Caroline* was a hive of activity. All manner of shapes and various sized boxes and packing crates were being loaded onboard. Outboard, ammunition was also being loaded from a lighter. Halting at the gangway he again showed his papers to the Royal Marine guard, who allowed him access to the ship. He saluted the White Ensign and stepped onto the holystoned wooden deck. The shout 'make way' sounded behind him, as a group of matelots rushed past, carrying some baulks of timber. The Quartermaster smiled. 'Nice to see a snotty put in his place,' he thought.

"Midshipman Alan Lee, reporting onboard, sir." He passed over his written orders, and he stood to attention in front of the Quartermaster lectern. "Thank you, sir, I will call the OOD."

"Brown, find the Gunnery Officer." A seaman scampered of to find the aforementioned. "First ship, sir?" the Qm asked.

"'er yes, I was on *Hannibal* for three weeks sea training, sir," stammered Lee.

The Qm rolled his eyes — another baby sailor onboard! "Don't call me sir. I work for a living, its Chief or PO, next time."

Lee flushed. He should have remembered that. "Err, sorry si— err, Chief."

The Qm rolled his eyes again. 'Roll on my twelve,' he thought.

While Lee waited, he looked at the ships crest, which was above her name board, HMS *Caroline* 1914 *Tenax Propositi* searching his memory for the Latin lessons he took, he remembered that it translated into "Tenacious of Purpose", how apt he thought.

That was a month ago, and now he was happily ensconced in the 'Gunroom'. There were twelve 'young gentlemen' who called this mess home. The leader of the mess was a nasty, overweight bully, called Sub-Lieutenant Tennent, who took particular delight in stealing other people's property. Lee became the Navigation Officers assistant, so he didn't spend much time in the Gunroom, so it saved him from the worst of Tennant's atrocities.

Being on the bridge, it did give Lee more insight into the role of the various officers and their duties. He could watch them go about their business, and how they treated the men. The Navigator was Lt Cdr Dave Vaughan, a reservist, who had been recalled to the flag for the duration. He was very good at his job, but could be a cantankerous individual at times, so Lee always approached him with caution. He taught Lee everything he knew, from 'shooting' the stars to updating the charts. Lee quickly learnt the art of being invisible when one of the officers or Captain was in a bad mood, a skill many 'young' gentlemen never mastered. His action station was in command of the Portside no 2 six-inch gun. He was fortunate he had a very good leading hand who knew all the tricks of his trade, and a few others as well!

Now they were in Scapa Flow, the Royal Navies bastion in the north, its huge windswept natural harbour, home to the officially named 'Grand Fleet', under Admiral Jellicoe, in his flagship *Iron Duke*. *Caroline* was the Leader of the 4th Destroyer Flotilla. She was responsible for twelve destroyers, and her role was to lead them into a torpedo attack on an enemy fleet, until then she provided an escort for the 'Grand Fleet' in the North Sea. This was good training for the rookie navigator; with the tricky tides, high winds and shifting sandbanks, he quickly became proficient at his trade. One day in spring, they were returning to Scapa, after another gruelling, fruitless patrol, having sighted nothing. Captain Crooke was in his usual position on the portside of the wheelhouse. After a short discussion with Vaughan, he turned and looked at Lee.

Beckoning him over, he said, "OK Mr Lee, take *Caroline* home, we will berth at our usual buoy, you have command of the ship," with that he turned and left the bridge.

Lee just stood there, mouth open, legs frozen. "Yes, sir," he stammered.

He felt a gentle hand on his shoulder. Vaughan said quietly in his ear, "It's OK, Mr Lee, I'm here, you can do this."

As they entered the Pentland Firth, where its currants and tide, were at their most aggressive, with the currant flowing one way and the wind blowing the other! Giving Muckle Skerry plenty of sea room, Lee ordered, "Starboard 35."

From the wheel, the Cox'n replied, "35 of wheel on, sir."

"Steady as you go, Cox'n... Midships." Lee was watching the bow like a hawk, *Caroline* was sliding down wind, and the currant was turning her faster than he wanted. He heard Vaughan suck air in through the gap in his teeth. Lee made his decision: "Slow ahead, Starboard engine, half ahead port." *Caroline* pivoted and entered through the boom at Flotta, as the boom defence drifter, scurried away to avoid any accidents. There was plenty of sea room. "Slow ahead both," Lee ordered as she moved across the sheltered waters of the Flow. Turning the ships head into wind, he ordered the whaler lowered and the 'buoy jumper', took the cable shackle. Once he was happy the ship was snugged down, he ordered, "Finish with main engines." Lee's knees went week — made it!

"Well done, Mr Lee," a loud voice behind him spoke. Turning, Captain Crooke was stood there. He had been behind the screen in the Chart room all the time. "Bring your journal to my cabin after evening meal, you have just qualified as watch keeper, well done. I shall get you an appointment on board *Iron Duke*, so you can sit your lieutenant's exam. Soon have your half stripe." He was beaming as he left the bridge.

Vaughan spoke in his ear, "Well done, boy, but don't ever enter the flow again at that speed. I have you in guts for garters if you do it again," and he laughed.

Lee passed his exam, and was promoted to Sub-lieutenant, much to the anger of Tennent, now of equal rank he could not bully Lee any more but took his anger out on the other midshipmen. *Caroline* transferred to the 2nd cruiser squadron, her role of leader of destroyers no longer needed, but still the patrols went on. By March 1916, her speed had dropped, and some minor repairs were needed, so they were sent to Newcastle for drydocking, some repairs, and having the ships bottom cleaned and painted. As a sign of his trust in Lee, the Captain let him plot a course to the Tyne, and to navigate most of the way there. Five days after her arrival, and snug in the drydock, German Zeppelins attacked the town. Lee led a party of seaman ashore to help with clearing the debris, recovering the dead, and helping the casualties, a very sobering experience for a young man.

On the 30th of May 1916, *Caroline* left Scapa, little did he know they were about to take part in the biggest naval clash since Trafalgar, The Battle of Jutland. She was now part of the 4th Light Cruiser Squadron; her role was to screen ahead of the Grand Fleet. In the late afternoon, Lee was at his action station on the P2 gun; he watched as Admiral Beattie's, Battle Cruisers Fleet, tore across the front of *Caroline* as the they headed toward the enemy battle fleet. Early evening, *HMS Caroline* was engaged by German destroyers, and his gun position was soon in the action, as they desperately tried to hit their elusive foe. She then came under fire from the German battleship *Nassau*, *Caroline* was straddled a few times by the battleship, and three of his gun crew were wounded, as shrapnel pinged of the gun mounting and bulkhead around them. The smell of cordite, and the fear would never leave him. As the action died down for the night, the ship's crew settled down to get some sleep, where they could at their action stations; it was likely they would be in action again in the morning. Around midnight, Lee, was awoken by a commotion at the next gun mounting P3, raised voices, and a large splash was heard. Lee moved down the deck to investigate. P3 gun mounting was Tennent's gun. There was a group of sailors stood by the rail, and personal items on the deck nearby.

"Where is Lieutenant Tennent?" Lee asked the Leading Seaman. The guns crew either looked away, or at the deck, or some part of the gun. Nobody would look him in the eye.

"Don't know, sir, haven't seen him for a bit," the L/S replied. Turning, he glared at his crew members.

Lee, "What's all this on the deck?" pointing at the items.

"Er nothing, sir, just having a swop of items." The L/S looked sheepish.

"Messenger go to the Gunroom and find the Lieutenant.

"You, Brown, go to the bridge and ask the No.1 to attend." Something was off here, so kick it up the chain of command, he thought, the ship ploughed on with her squadron mates as they searched for the German High Sea Fleet. After an extensive search, no trace of the Sub Lieutenant was ever found onboard, his 'ditty' box had been opened, and the contents spread all over the Gunroom Lobby.

Lee and the rest of the two-gun crews were interviewed by the 'Master at Arms' and the Captain, but no explanation was forth coming. There was little point in searching back along their track; the North Sea was bitterly cold, so if he went overboard, he had little chance of survival.

Years later, when working in the Admiralty building, Lee found out that Tennent had been stealing from his messmates, and other members of his gun crew. Summary action had been taken that cold night on the North Sea; many items were returned to their owners. In the ship's log, Tennent was reported 'DD' (Discharged Dead) during the Battle of Jutland. The one thing that sailors cannot stand is a thief and a bully!

Late December 1916, Lee received his orders. He was to proceed to Dover to join the Tribal class destroyer *Mohawk*, as navigating officer; he also received his other half stripe. Now officially Lieutenant Alan Lee. So, it was with some sadness he left *Caroline*, leaving behind Captain Crooke, Lt. Vaughan and the rest of the ships company. This would be a different kind of war — no more boring patrols, finding nothing, and long days moored in windswept Scapa.

Chapter 9

One month later, his ships and crews were rested and refitted. His aircraft had been replaced and brought up to date, the "acquired" aircraft still safely stowed in the lower hanger, out of sight, out of mind. Two Walrus aircraft were now onboard *Georgic* — they would prove useful for Search and Rescue, a service he needed badly. New pilots and aircrew had joined. The force had also been joined by *HMAS Darwin*, an Apollo class cruiser, who's skipper, Commander Steve "Digger" Dawson, was keen as mustard, and raring to go.

It was a misty morning as they made their departure from Sydney, one month later, and back to the war. His destroyers had left first to throw an anti- submarine screen out to protect the big ships. Earlier in the war the Japanese sub fleet had made an unsuccessful attack on Sydney, so they were still around. They headed out due east, across the Tasman Sea; they were heading for Wellington in New Zealand 'to show the flag' — to let the Kiwis know that the navy was around to protect them. Lee watched as his force took up their steaming stations. *Georgic* launched its patrol aircraft, and the supply ships bringing up the rear. He was very disappointed: twelve of his sailors had gone

AWOL, mostly off *Wren* and *Empire Brecon*. They spent the time getting the crews back into shape and dusting of the cobwebs and lethargy, that too much time in port creates.

As they approached the Cook Straight, two New Zealand Minesweepers were there to greet him, and escort the force into Wellington harbour. There was not enough berth space for the whole force so *Georgic* and *Kent* berthed in the bay. Lee made his official round of meetings. The second day was for a children's party to be held on *Stockport*, *Bellona*, and *Lavish*. This was a great success. Lee noticed the Buffer and Chief Stoker had made a carousel to fit on the capstan, which was very popular with every one, apart from the stokers, who had to keep steam up for the capstan!

The following day they sailed. Again west, a Japanese force had been reported off Fiji, and they were off to investigate. He ordered *Darwin, Meteor*, and *Myngs* to divert slightly and check out the Chatham Islands. An Avenger was also sent to inspect the islands, and make sure the small Naval party based there were OK. They now entered the Pacific Ocean. The sea turned to a deeper blue with a long slow swell to it. The radar and lookouts reported clear of any ships or aircraft. Once the Chatham's had reported clear and *Myngs* had dropped of supplies. They headed north towards Tonga; their mission was to attack the airfield on Tonga, as they headed for Fiji. This time, Lee insisted on better reconnaissance of the target and more fighters in the strike force. Also, he would take

Stockport, *Kent* and *Darwin* closer in and assist with a bombardment, using their 8 and 6in guns. This time two Avengers were launched, and arrived undetected, and where able to make a better report.

Lt. Steve Wood had been made Senior Pilot following the loss of his friend Dave Johnson. He would make sure things would be better this time. He stressed that when strafing an airfield, they would only make one pass; it was obvious that two or more passes increased significantly the chances of being shot down. The airfield had fourteen 'Betty' bombers, twenty Zeros and about a dozen 'Rufe' fighters on the slipway. These were Zeros fitted with floats, despite their looks were very manoeuvrable and had a very long range. Although his fighters had been replaced, they now carried the Wildcat V. It was becoming obvious that were being outmatched by the latest Japanese fighters. They had been promised, newer and better fighters, a version of the Spitfire was one, now called a Seafire, it was eagerly awaited. Before the strike force had assembled over the carrier, *Stockport*, *Kent* and *Darwin* had departed to form a Gun Line off the coast of Tonga. They approached under the cover of darkness; their gun spotting Avengers had launch earlier and were now circling awaiting daylight. The strike force were minutes away when the sun peeped over the horizon.

The plan was *Stockport*, *Kent* and *Darwin* would fire five full gun salvos, then pause to allow the fighters to strafe, followed by the Bombers to crater the runway and hangers, then they would re-open fire and finish off anything remaining. As Lee sat on his bridge chair, with his anti-flash gear on, he could feel the sweat trickling down his back. The radio repeater was on and he could hear the spotters giving out range and bearing for his Gun Director. "Tango 1 to Father, your first target is airport control tower, range 10,000 yards, green 97 degrees."

"DCT... Bridge, permission to open fire."

Lee spoke, "Permission granted."

"Commence, commence, commence." Ting ting.

Bang! and the bridge shook, cordite fumes blew across the ship.

"Tango 1 to father, in line, down 100 shoot!"

Ting ting, Bang!

"Tango 1 to Father on target, shoot."

After the five salvos, the ship went silent, allowing the aircraft took over the strike. He could see the explosions in the distance as the bombers unloaded their deadly cargoes. He also saw the fighters go in low down, then rise into the skies, their part done. "Tango 1," came back on air "Father new target..." And so, it went on for the next fifteen minutes until there was nothing left the destroy. The aircraft returned to *Big G*; there was no losses, and only damage to one Avenger. The gun line increased speed and rejoined the force, then they all headed north.

The next day, Lee judged he was far enough away from Tonga. He refuelled his ships, this took all day, but they all now had full tanks. The following day *Georgic* went along side *Rover* and refilled her petrol stowage. Lee was contented, as a young midshipman onboard *Caroline*, he had been told "that wars were not won by battles, but by logistics" something he remembered!

For the next few days, they headed north, towards Fiji. Lee was in his sea cabin, doing the never-ending paperwork, when there was a knock on the door. It was Dave Vickers. "OK Mr Vickers, sit down. What have you got for me?"

"Thank you, sir, we have picked up signals from the northeast. Using the latest code books from the Yanks, we have determined that there is a Japanese carrier force between Fiji and Pago Pago, heading N W towards the Solomon Islands. We feel that this is the force we have been sent out to locate."

Lee took a look at his chart, leaned across and picked up the bridge phone. "Bridge… Captain here, alter course due west, until further notice, signal the force.

"OK, Dave, can you work out what we would be up against from the signals?"

"It will take time, but we think so," came the reply.

"Very good, keep me updated, good work."

Captain Sumio Suzuki was stood at his bridge chair, watching the aircraft carrier *Shinyo*, as she completed her aircraft recovery and fell in astern of his heavy cruiser, *Kako*. What he had been watching made him shake his head: what was the Captain of *Shinyo* doing? It was taking far too long to land and stow aircraft. Twelve months ago, His Imperial Japanese Navy had the finest and best trained air fleets in the world, but with the losses suffered during Operation I-Go the attack on Midway, and the decimation of aircraft in the Bismarck, and Coral Seas, meant he now had a cargo ship conversion as a carrier and partially trained aircrews. He hoped that the Yankees would give them enough time to train these aircrews up. That was the reason they were so far south, to give them some combat experience attacking the small French islands of French Polynesia.

At least his cruisers and destroyers' forces were still undiluted and remained a very potent force. His gaze fell across *Aoba*. She was commanded by his friend and ex classmate Toni Wakanabi. He viewed his destroyers, all Special service '*Fubuki*' class, *Fubuki* herself, *Miyuki*, *Oboro* and *Sagiri*. Following the battles near Savo Island in the Solomon's, he wanted to get revenge on the Yankees. He sighed. For now he had to settle for nursemaiding this group of children. He dispatched a signal to Headquarters, reporting fuel remaining and the possibility of a tanker, and the estimated time of arrival at Rabaul, then retired for a bowl of noodles and a glass of sake.

Lee's phone rang. "Captain, sir, can you come to the code room, please?" the urgent voice of the CPO in charge asked.

Lee was awake. "On my way."

Once inside he noticed that it was significantly cooler in there; the Buffer and some of his deck crew had rigged up a very effective wind scoop that channelled air in to the area. "Ah that's better," he said out loud. "OK, Chief, what have you got for me?"

"Sir, we have intercepted a signal, and decoded most of it. There is a force of Jap warships to the northeast of us, heading back to Rabaul. It comprises of a Carrier, the *Shinyo*, a cruiser, the *Aoba* and four Fubuki class destroyers, and possible another warship. We can't find her in the code books that the US Navy gave us."

"If the figures are correct then the destroyers are all short of fuel, and are trying to conserve it, they have asked for a tanker."

"Thanks, Chief, well done, see if you can find any more Japs in the area."

Well, well, could we do it. He left the cabin with multiple scenarios going through his head. He headed straight for the chart table, beckoning Andy Watson to join him. Much later, he made a call to Pat Byrne and his Senior Pilot Andy Wood.

The following morning, an area search to the NE was launched from *Big G* to look for the enemy. Lee was in his cabin going over his plans again, when a knock at the door, opened by Andy, with a big smile on his face. "Found 'em."

Lt Joey Smyth was sat in just his shorts; the heat though the canopy made the sweat run down his chest. Looking out of his bullet proof windscreen, he spotted something flash. What was that? He turned his big, safe Avenger bomber in that direction. Ships, he could see ships! He looked for a suitable cloud to hid in, while the Observer worked out their position. Once he had done so, he left the cover of the cloud and started to count the ships.

He then ducked back into cover. This was repeated a few times until he was happy; he had all the information. His Radio operator then sent a long message passing all the information to *Big G*; once he had done that, he settled down to shadow the enemy. The information was passed from *Georgic* to *Stockport*, and the proper briefing could commence. Another Avenger was launched to take over the spotting duties, as Smyth's aircraft was running low on fuel. From the signals coming from the spotting aircraft, it would appear that the carrier was conducting training, as the aircraft were seen to take off did a few circuits then landed again. This was good news for Lee. Later that day, Lee left the force with *Stockport, Kent, Darwin* and all the destroyers. He left *Bellona* to give AA protection to the supply force and *Georgic*. He wanted to close the Jap force to be ready to attack at dawn.

Georgic's strike force fell upon the enemy ships just as the sun peeped over the horizon. The aircraft's orders were carrier first. It was a maximum effort; every available aircraft was in the air. In a manoeuvre straight out of the textbook, the torpedo bombers attacked from either side of the bow, while the bombers struck from above. All the fighters circled overhead. Lee had gambled that there was no real threat to his supply force, so used them all. Even the two Walrus aircraft were used for rescue work.

On *Shinyo*, the wail of the action stations siren woke him up. The Captain hastily got dressed and reached for the cabin door. He felt as though his feet were a double thud, then he was hit by a pressure wave as three bombs penetrated his wooden flight deck. This was the last thing he felt on this earth, as his spirit left to meet his ancestors. One torpedo had hit the port bow, and another starboard side abreast the forward boiler room. The three bombs hit all on the centre line and exploded in the forward hanger, engine room and after magazine.

Like *Georgic*, *Shinyo* was a converted merchant ship. Her conversion had been that hurried; she had not had extra watertight bulkheads added, armour fitted to her Petrol tanks or firefighting equipment fitted, so she could not stand up to this onslaught. Her main armament would have been her aircraft, but they were all safely tucked away in her hanger. The Captain thinking he was in safe waters. A fatal mistake. This was an attack, straight out of the training manual!

Once it was clear that the carrier was finished the last ten Avengers concentrated on the cruisers, three with torpedoes the rest with bombs. To add to the confusion, the Wildcats made a mass strafing attack on the remaining warships. Captain Suzuki was rooted to the spot: that fool, I told him to have aircraft ready to launch at dawn! It was too late now. He had more important matters; his ship *Kako* was under air attack. A string of 500lb bombs landed alongside the ship, peppering the sides with shrapnel. Two destroyers, *Fubuki* and *Miyuki*, had made their way to assist *Shinyo*. All eyes were on the aircraft attack, and the sinking carrier.

In the days before Radar Ranging and reliable radios fitted to spotting aircraft, it would have taken five or six salvos before you were able to get the range on an enemy opponent. Lee thought, not now, for three years of this war, the Royal Navy had taken a pounding, and lost many fine ships, but not now, now it was our turn. "Bridge... Guns, target the right-hand cruiser," Lee ordered.

He could hear over the radio repeater, the conversation between Ives and the spotting aircraft. "DCT... Bridge, permission to open fire?"

Lee, "Open Fire."

"Enemy ships in sight to the southwest."

The shout paralyzed *Kako's* Bridge personnel for a split second. Suzuki ran to the bridge wing, to see one, three funnel heavy cruiser, one Town and a Leander class English cruisers and destroyers, the cruisers in a gun line, the destroyers deploying for a torpedo attack — why hadn't the lookouts spotted them? As he watched, out of the corner of his eye, he saw *Aoba* shuddered as she was hit by two 8in armoured piercing shells. His view was obstructed as columns of dirty brown water, rose towards the heavens, and his ship shuddered.

He shouted at the bridge in general: "All ships, commence torpedo attack."

Kako shuddered as the ship was hit again; this time by a mixture of light and heavy shells. *Aoba* hauled out of line; her intension was to divide the enemy ships. The close escort of *Oboro* and *Sagiri* turned and raced toward the attacking enemy. *Fubuki* and *Miyuki*, were further away, but they left their rescue mission, and headed to join their squadron mates. *Kako* shuddered again, hit by more shells. Her control tower was wrecked, only one of the aft turrets could fire. He was taking in water in the stern gland space, and the aft engine room also right forward in the paint locker, which was giving off, black obnoxious fumes. Suzuki knew his ship was doomed; his Torpedo officer reported they had managed to fire eight torpedoes, the rest were wrecked. The ship shuddered again, more hits. The steering was destroyed; the ship would not answer the helm.

As professional sailor, he was impressed by the British cruisers fire. They seemed to be able to hit with each shell, something His Imperial Majesties ships could not manage. It was clear they did not have long, so Suzuki ordered the Emperor's portrait to be placed in a boat for safety, then told his crew to abandon ship. He himself would go down with the ship in the finest tradition of the navy. The ship was hit again, and he was knocked out. He awoke as his sailors were pulling him into a life raft!

Stockport shuddered. She had been hit aft, the sea blossomed around her, with multicoloured water, as the Japanese ships used a different coloured shell, for correcting the fall of shot. *Kent* took a direct hit on her bridge structure, causing many deaths.

On *Aoba*, she was fighting for her life, hit repeatedly by armour piercing shells, and a final attack by a lone Avenger bomber which put a bomb straight down the ships funnel, which exploded in the boiler rooms. This brought the ship to a stop. The two destroyers *Oboro* and *Sagiri* tried to lay a smoke screen between *Aoba* and the enemy.

They were strafed by the Wildcats, then *Sagiri*, disappeared under a deluge of eight-inch shells. *Oboro* turned to port, her port side shredded by six-inch shell fire, both destroyers were doomed. The two remaining destroyers were racing to catch up, when *Fubuki*, suddenly slowed down; she had stripped a turbine, she hauled away and started to lay smoke. *Miyuki* stayed on course to attack. In line abreast the British destroyers open fire on their outnumbered adversary. It was a very unequal fight; hit repeatedly by 4.7-inch shells and a torpedo from *Lavish*, she slowly stopped and started to sink by the stern. Her bows rising above her survivor's heads, as she disappeared beneath the waves.

Lee was watching. The much-vaunted Japanese cruiser and destroyer force had been decimated by the Royal and Australian navies.

"Torpedo in sight, off the port bow," shouted the lookout. *Kako's* torpedoes were nearing the end of their journey.

Lee, "Hard a port" — those damn Jap torpedoes! "Full astern port shaft, full ahead starboard shaft." Lee was desperately trying to bring *Stockport's* bow round. "Bunts, warn the rest of the force!"

One torpedo disappeared under the overhang at the bow. Lee held his breath. It came back in sight, missed. A collective sigh went up from the bridge. *Kent* was not so lucky; it struck her stern with a terrific explosion, as "X" and "Y" magazines erupted. "Signal, *Meteor* and *Lookout*, standby *Kent*."

"Order an Anti-submarine screen to the destroyers, tell *Georgic* to launch an anti-sub aircraft." The orders flowed. "*Darwin* wants to know should she finish off the last destroyer." "Message from *Kent*, many casualties." "*Myngs* reporting damage and casualties." "*Georgic* reporting three aircraft missing." And so, it went on.

Lee was exhausted; he had nodded off twice while sat in his bridge chair. After looking at the updated "butchers bill", he said a silent prayer to the dead. He stood up to stretch his legs and wake himself up. He looked around the bridge the fatigue was palpable. Looking aft he watched as the buffer and his deck crew continued making repairs to the shell damage. He took his binoculars and looked at his force. To starboard, *Darwin* had *Kent* under tow; she was down by the stern with a 10-degree list to starboard, her engine rooms flooded, rudder and propeller shafts destroyed, she kept yawing to port. Her bridge twisted and blackened. It was a tribute to her builders and her 'black gang' that she was still afloat. *Myngs* was following her astern, her Engine room staff, desperately trying to keep the sea out of the one remaining engine room. *Bellona* had transferred additional salvage pumps and her Doctor to *Myngs* to assist with the dead and dying. It had been three days since the battle, and he met his supply ships yesterday. Now it was a long slow tow back to Sydney. The aircrew on *Georgic*, despite being very tired, were gallantly putting up aircraft to protect them. He had stopped the force this morning. It was a calculated risk, but he had all the wounded from *Stockport*, *Kent*, *Myngs*, and

Lavish transferred to *Empire Brecon* — she had better facilities for dealing with them. *Georgic* had a good medical ward, so she could look after her own. He also took the opportunity to refuel and resupply the force, and lastly bury the dead.

His signal team had been inundated with congratulations and best wishes. He knew that they were famous when 'Tokyo Rose' mentioned them on her broadcasts; fortunately she did not know names off the force's ships, but 'threatened death to all Tommies'. They continued west, Sydney had signalled that they were sending two Ocean going salvage tugs and some Minesweepers and Patrol sloops to assist. Five days later, they met up with the tugs, who took over the tow from a grateful *Darwin*. Poor *Myngs* was doomed; her crew had tried to keep her afloat, but the cruel sea had finally won. Just as the tugs hove in sight, Lee ordered her abandoned, and she slipped slowly below the waves.

It took another five long days for Force 'Y' to pass the Heads, and into Sydney. The news of their arrival had obviously got around, every vantage point was full of well-wishers, the loudest roar of all, was for *Darwin*. *Georgic, Bellona* and *Stockport* again berthed at Garden Island. Along with the destroyers, *Kent* was towed to Cockatoo Island. She was so badly damaged she would never sail again. *Empire Brecon* discharged her patients to a fleet of ambulances, and a repair team from the dockyard swarmed onboard *Stockport*. Lee was exhausted but had to make the usual round of official visits, everybody wanting a debrief off the trip, official receptions were laid on for the crews. Lee insisted that the crews on *Brecon* and *Rover* were also invited, after all they were part of the team.

Chapter 10

Ten days later, they were repaired and rested, when the sailing orders arrived. The Americans had been taking a beating at a place called Guadalcanal. Lee was to proceed to join the American forces, to try to interdict Japanese cruiser and destroyers from Rabaul, who were trying to resupply the last few remaining Japanese troops, that were holed up on the island. Although the island had officially been declared clear of the enemy, a few soldiers were still launching raids on the airstrip, known as Henderson Field. The bulk of the American fleet had moved on to other duties — this problem needed sorting out. There were no replacement ships, so Lee had to depart with the ships under his command. However, somebody had been listening; his aircraft losses were made good, and additional aircrew supplied. As they left harbour the ships spread out into cruising formation, and the usual air patrol was launched. They headed to the northeast and increased speed to *Brecon's* maximum. After a few terse messages to the Admiralty in London, about his lack of ships, he received the message that the New Zealand cruiser, *HMNZS Leander* would be joining him later. It was better than nothing. So, he conducted exercises to get everybody back into shape, the hot spots of Sydney were too good to miss, but the crews needed the cobwebs removing and to be back up to speed. One week later, his air patrol reported a warship closing from the west; it was soon identified as the Kiwi cruiser, *Leander*, whose Captain was an old classmate of Lee's, Ray Westcott.

"Bunts, signal *Leander*, message "It's a long way from Britannia."

A few moments later, "*Leander* replying, sir. If I had known you were here, I would not have come. Proud to serve under you!" Lee smiled.

Andy Watson moved over to Lee's chair. "You know him long, sir?" he asked.

"Yes, No 1, we were at Britannia together. He's a damn good cruiser skipper, one of the best ship handlers I have ever seen. I can also guarantee his crew will be top notch, not as good as us, but OK." They both laughed. One of the bridge lookouts was watching the exchange and stated to relax; 'If the Old Man and Jimmy were laughing', all was right with the world. *Leander* took up her assigned station.

"Message, sir, *Leander* requests refuelling from *Rover*."

"Approved."

Another signal sir from '*Big G*' — Lee smiled, that nickname had stuck! "Report of submarine on the surface, due east, fifty miles, request to launch a strike."

Lee, "Approved."

"Too late, sir, sub dived."

"Very good, ask the patrol to sit on the contact, for as long as fuel holds out."

"I think it's about time that *Magpie* and *Wren* had some fun; ask them to take a look see," Lee ordered. *Stockport's* bridge crew could almost hear the whoop of delight as the two sloops, headed off at top speed, to do what they do best, hunt subs.

Onboard *Wren*, her skipper Lt Cmdr. J.P.L. Desprez, a French destroyer Captain, who had thrown in his lot with the RN when France fell. Was glad to go and hunt the sub, his ship had already sunk three German U-Boats, the ships mixed French and British crew had settled down, after some initial problems and were now a well-drilled, killing team. But he wanted more. He looked across at his opposite number on *Magpie*; Sean Kelly, the red haired, fiery Irishman from Belfast, was stood on the bridge wing, urging his ship on. They could see the Avenger aircraft on the horizon, and she reported that the sub was trailing oil, so was easy to follow. Between themselves, they had a routine. After contact *Wren* would hold the target on ASDIC and *Magpie* would attack, the roles would then reverse. *Yoke 1* reported she was low on fuel, so after passing on details, departed the scene.

Onboard the 400-ton, Imperial Japanese Army submarine *Yu7*, the Captain, Lt. Suki, was furious after dropping off supplies at that god forsaken atoll. The Navigator had managed to hit the reef, when leaving the lagoon. Now his boat was leaking diesel fuel and had a damaged propeller, which was making a loud noise, and the sub could only proceed slowly. He had spotted the American Avenger aircraft, and ordered the dive, not one of the blind lookouts even saw it. His submarine was his first command, but he hated it. It had been built to supply outlying garrisons, and was not built for warfare; it had a deck gun, which was not much use and no torpedo tubes, so he was just a delivery truck, crewed by twenty-three idiots, this was not what he joined the Army for. He ordered the sub up to periscope depth, and took a look, that plane was still there. He made a quick sweep of the horizon. He could not believe his eyes: two destroyers coming straight towards him. "Crash dive, take us down," he screamed. "Turn to Starboard, full ahead." At 4 ½ knots he was not going to outrun anybody.

"Bridge... Asdic, loud propeller noises crossing right to left depth 400 ft."

"Target is very noisy and slow, no down doppler!" Captain Desprez smiled: got him. "Pass on to *Magpie*, bearing, depth and speed, No1, slow *Wren* to 10 knots, follow the plot."

"*Magpie* signaling, attacking."

Everyone on the upper deck watched as *Magpie,* with a large black flag flying from her port yardarm dropped twelve 500lbs Depth Charges, filled with Amatol explosives. Twelve huge fountains of dirt brown water, clawed skywards, only to collapse down again. The crash and bang could be felt through their seaboots as *Magpies* first attack died away. Now it was *Wrens* turn; she changes course and increased speed. Attacking, again the 'I am prosecuting Submarine' Black Flag streaming from her yardarm. This went on for thirty minutes, each taking it in turn. After *Wren* last attack, a huge bubble rose to the surface and burst; it was full of debris, a hammock, a couple of books, lifejacket, part of a man's torso, bits of uniforms. Then followed a large and spreading pool of fuel. *Magpie* launched a sea boat to collect evidence of the sinking, while *Wren* launched a boat to start collecting the dead fish, for a fish supper.

A short while later they headed back to rejoin Force 'Y'. A patrol Avenger arrived overhead to escort them home. Lee was in his cabin, when the phone rang. "Sir, *Magpie* and *Wren* in sight, signalling enemy sunk!"

"Very good, I will come up." On the bridge, as the sloops were getting closer, "Signalman, order *Magpie* and *Wren* to resume positions, but to pass through the force," and "to all ships, cheer *Wren* and *Magpie*."

It was two very happy ships companies, as they acknowledged each ships thunderous cheers, when it was *Stockport's* turn, Lee stood on the bridge wing and waved his cap with a lot of enthusiasm. They resumed the positions in the screen, then from *Stockport* a signal: "Well done, *Magpie* and *Wren*. Splice the Main Brace."

Later, sat in his bridge chair, Lee watched as a jackstay transfer took place, between *Wren* and *Magpie*, and smiled; the fish was being shared out. Backhouse, the navigator approached his chair. "Sir, can you look at the chart? We are approaching the Solomon's… and when you have a minute, Mr Vickers would like to see you in the code room." They both moved to the chart table. Backhouse continued, "The information we have from the Yanks is to enter during daylight between Guadalcanal and Savo Island, and to enter the fleet anchorage in something they call 'Ironbottom Sound', but that's not on any of our charts, so it might need us to ask when we get there."

"Thanks Pilot, plot me a course, and speed to get us there in daylight."

"I shall go and see our 'little wizard' in the code room." They both laughed at Mr Vickers unofficial nickname.

As he approached the code room, the marine sentry came to attention. Lee smiled. "You on duty again, Marine Bennett? Have you been in trouble?"

"Err well sir, it was..."

"That's OK, Bennett, relax." He smiled and went into the code office. Bennett relaxed. "One of the better skippers," he sighed.

The CPO spotted Lee entering. "Morning, sir," he called. This was to wake everybody up.

Lee smiled. "It's OK, Chief, let them relax."

Dave Vickers came out of a side cabin, with a sheet of paper in his hand. "Hello sir, thanks for coming down."

Lee, "OK sub, what have you got?"

"Well sir, I think we know the name of the sub the sloops got. Rabaul have been transmitting on a regular basis for *YU7,* apparently it is a Jap Army sub, and it's not responding; it appears all other call signs have acknowledged. I didn't know the Jap Army had their own subs, that's a bit unusual, sir."

"Neither did I, Sub. Pass it on to the Americans, Sydney and the Admiralty, would you?"

"Aye, sir."

"Anything else?"

"With the information we received, there is a strong force operating out of Rabaul, under the orders of one Captain Tanaka; apparently he is one of their top-notch commanders. We are still trying to determine his strength, but being in harbour, they are not using their radios much. We do know that the heavy cruiser, *Takao* left Singapore one week ago and has now arrived in Rabaul, but she is reporting engine problems. We will update you when we can fill in any more gaps."

Lee smiled. "Chief, any tea in that fanny? I am parched."

There he stayed for an hour, just talking to the men, and getting a feel for their mood. It was well worth the hour spent; these were well motivated and intelligent men. He will mention them all in his next message to London.

The following morning, they exchanged signals with the lookout position at Veranaaso on Guadalcanal, just as two destroyer escorts came around the headland to escort them to the anchorage. The lead destroyer signalled a greeting, then a constant blizzard of messages: 'saying how good it was to see them, he had been in London, once, did he know such and such.' It just went on and on, until one of the Telegraphists said, "I wish he would shut up, he's making my eyes ache." This brought laughter on the bridge. As they passed between Guadalcanal and Savo Island, the fleet anchorage opened out in front of him. There was two Fletcher class Destroyers, who were guarding the gap between Savo and Guadalcanal, moved aside to give them sea room, and welcomed them.

A small patrol boat came along side with a US Navy Commander onboard. He was to direct them to the ships berth. He was complete with tin helmet, lifejacket, binoculars and a big message pouch. On entering the bridge on *Stockport*, he saluted and asked permission to come aboard, a complete change from the last US Navy Commander he met. As he stood on the compass platform, looking to take up *Stockport's* berth, they felt rather than heard a zing! And a bullet ricocheted off the guardrail and hit the DCT and landed at Lee's feet.

"What the hell," Watson said.

As cool as you could be, the US Commander turned, "Damn snipers, at it again, Captain, please tell your men to take care when on the upper deck; they like to take potshots at sailors in white!"

Once they were berthed, Alan escorted the officer down to his cabin for a drink, a rare treat, American warships were 'dry'. British warships were always popular for social visits, and to take delivery of the message pouch. Lee asked where Iron bottom Sound was. As it was not marked on the charts. He laughed, "Gee Captain, your berthed in it. We have lost so many ships here, that the seabed is littered with wrecks. Somebody had the bright idea to call it Ironbottom Sound! Too many good ships and men have died for that name!" They raised their glasses. "Absent friends."

At 0900 sharp, Lee presented himself, along with Pat Byrne, Lt Steve Wood, Ray Arnold, Steve Dawson, all-in full-dress whites, out of sight of the land, on the quarterdeck of the American flagship, the USS *Pensacola*. There they were met by a U.S. Marines Guard of Honour and a small band. The Admiral, Silvester Issacs, and Captain Theo Goodman, the skipper of the *Pensacola*, stepped forward to great them. "Welcome aboard, Captain, how nice it is to meet you, would you like to inspect the Guard?" This took Lee aback; he had never inspected a guard before! "Sir." Ah well in for a penny… It was a surreal experience, in the distance he could hear the crump of mortars, and the stutter of machine gunfire, and listening to the 'put-put' sound of landing craft going about their business. After the inspection, they retired to the Admirals Stateroom to discuss strategy.

On entering the stateroom, Lee handed a bottle each of Scotch Whiskey to Issacs and Goodman. This unexpected gift was a pleasant surprise for the American officers. Here was a no-nonsense Admiral; he got straight down to it. "Captain, can you transfer your aircraft to Henderson Field to assist in strike operations and a CAP over the fleet?" Lee looked at Pat and Steve Wood. They both nodded.

"Yes, sir, I will need to send *Georgic* to sea to catch a wind." He could see Pat and Steve nodding again. "But not a problem."

"Good, can your frigates back up the sub patrols between 'The Canal', Savo and Tulagi?"

"Again sir, not a problem."

"Also I will need your cruisers and destroyers to form a strike force, to try and stop these supply runs by 'The Tokyo Express'." He went on, "Use your own fuel and supplies for now, but if you run short of fuel etc., just draw it from us, understood?"

"Finally, I might need your carrier to act as an aircraft transport. We are short of aircraft and if we can transport more into here, we will stand a better chance of winning, and finally, Captain, how many men under your command?"

That stunned Alan, he had no idea. "About 5000, I think, sir. I can get an update in a few minutes... why?"

The Admiral smiled. "Please do that. At 1800 hours today we will deliver enough Bar-B-Cued steak for every member of your force courtesy of the US Navy."

"Wow," was all they said at once.

The Admiral smiled and reaching for a glass of whiskey. "Now, Captain Lee, tell me about sinking Nip cruisers!"

Later that day, *Georgic*, escorted by *Wren*, *Magpie* and *Lavish* sailed to find open water, then to launch all her aircraft. They all landed at Henderson Field. They then returned to the anchorage. She also offloaded the two

Walrus in case they were needed. Sure, enough at 1800, a fleet of landing craft delivered hot steaks to every British ship in the anchorage.

Next morning, Lee stood on the quarterdeck as he watched *Georgic*, escorted by two destroyer escorts and a Fletcher class destroyer, leave for Bora Bora to load new aircraft. He had a lump in his throat. He hoped nothing would go wrong. He would miss her 'ugly' shape. He was interrupted by Mr Vickers: "Excuse me, sir."

"That's OK, Dave, what's up?"

"I have been to the flagship and got updated info. They knew about the Jap Army subs but didn't know they were around here. They also gave me our orders for tonight; there is a reported run of Jap destroyers down 'The Slot' tonight, but I checked the info… I think there is a cruiser with them. The intel guys say I am wrong, but I know I am right." Vickers looked annoyed.

"OK, Dave, I will speak to the yanks. Are we ordered to intercept them?"

"Sir, I think so, but it's addressed to you."

A little later in his day cabin, Lee opened his orders. He was to sail at mid-day; all his ships, plus three US destroyers, were to sail north to a certain spot and lie in wait for the enemy destroyers to appear. He got on the TBS to Captain Goodman. "Hi Theo, could you get onto your intel guys, ask them to check the info they have passed just in case they have missed anything? Also, I don't think it's a good idea for the three US destroyers to sail with us; we haven't worked together yet and I don't want any mistakes to happen?"

"Good idea, Alan, we will leave them in here, and I will update the admiral, good hunting!"

Lee spent the next few hours studying the battle reports from the Americans. They used predictable tactics, so he planned something different. Once he formulated his own plan, he then spoke to the other Captains.

Later as the force split, he wished them good luck. He watched as *Leander, Darwin, Lookout* and *Lively* headed to the northeast to hide in the Manning strait, between Wagina Island and Santa Isabella Island. He took *Bellona, Meteor* and *Lavish* to the northwest to linger in the Kula Gulf, north of New Georgia. Both forces had made good time and were able to take up their stations before the sun set. In the code room, Dave Vickers and his 'secret squirrels' sat at their receivers waiting for enemy transmissions. The sun disappeared in a blood red glow over the horizon. All ships now closed up at action stations, their radar aerials searching the ether for any activity, and they waited.

Onboard *Georgic*, Pat Byrne looked around his command: all was quiet, with the aircrew missing it was like a school without the children. He had embarked two 'war weary' Wildcat fighters from Henderson to give a bit of protection. They would be dropped off at Bora Bora, probably for scrapping. He looked aft towards them, a poor pair of specimens, he thought. He stood on the bridge gratings and looked at his escorts. They looked competent enough. Then he looked ahead. The sky was dark and foreboding; they were in for a blow. Later that night, a storm force eight gale fell across the ships. For two days, they fought the storm. *Georgic's* hull, being made for ocean cruising, fared well, however one of the Wildcats, broke her lashing, and disappeared over the side. The destroyers took it badly, and one of the DE's disappeared into the gloom.

Two days later, they entered the lagoon into Bora Bora, the boom defence vessel giving *Big G* a toot on her whistle. She was taken in tow and positioned alongside the wharf at Vailtape. He looked around the lagoon — this was America's industry at maximum output, ships of all shapes and sizes were present, the wharfs and airfield packed with brand new aircraft. In the lagoon was Catalina flying boats, moored in a long line. No time was wasted, as an oiler was brought along side, and cranes began loading brand new, Hellcats, Corsairs, and Avenger aircraft and a fleet of trucks and jeeps, so new you could smell the fresh paint.

Taking a leaf out of Lee's play book, Pat and his No1 went ashore with a crate of whiskey to find the officer in charge of the depot. Shortly after they returned to *Big G*, a young officer appeared, with authorization for six brand new Jeeps all painted in RN markings. They would make light work on the flight, and hanger decks — why push an airplane, when you can get a jeep to tow it, whiskey well spent. These were quickly stowed out of sight. The work went on all night, until every nook and granny filled with aircraft, vehicles, and packing crates of every size and shape. Pat was worried. *Georgic* was well overloaded. So, he got an American launch, and sailed around the hull to check the waterline. The missing DE had shown up, but badly damaged by the storm, so she was left behind and *Georgic* sailed with the other two escorts back to Guadalcanal. Thankfully the sea was benign, and the enemy left them alone.

To the north, just as the moon began to rise, the tannoy spoke, "Radar... Bridge movement to the north, sir."

"Captain here, what do you see?" Lee looked to the north, but his view was obstructed by bulk of Kolombangara island.

"We can see two similar shapes and one bigger. If we had to guess, two destroyers and a cruiser."

"Excellent, well done." Lee was thinking hard, this was what he had hoped for. He would let them pass the bay entrance, once clear he would follow them, staying close inshore. When he was happy, they would open fire. But if *Leander's* group were in the line of fire he would wait. When ready, they would both open fire together. This would trap the enemy between them. But it was a risk; he had to be careful of 'Friendly fire'. Three dark shapes, sailing in line ahead passed the entrance of Kula Gulf, the white bow wave made a contrast for the Gun Director to take ranges, this backed up his radar ranging.

On the radar repeater Lee could see the enemy force passing ahead and he could also see *Leander's* force emerges from her hiding place. When 'Guns' was happy, he asked permission to fire. Only recently Force 'Y' had been supplied with 'flashless cordite'. This was the first time he had used it. The command was given: "Open Fire."

"Commence, commence, commence."

Stockport shuddered as the first salvo was released. *Bellona* fired three 'starshells' — these burst above the enemy force, illuminating them. The lookout could now see two enemy destroyers, their decks packed with 50gallon drums. These were ready to be dropped into the ocean for the tide to wash them ashore for the soldiers to recover. The middle ship was another *Tama* class light cruiser. She felt the full force of Force 'Y''s guns. *Stockport's* second salvo did the damage, hit by five 6in shells. The cruiser shuddered to a stop, then *Leander* and *Darwin* also found the range. *Darwin* soon shifted target and engaged the last destroyer, while *Bellona* took on the lead destroyer. *Stockport* stopped firing, while *Leander* joined *Bellona* in pounding the lead destroyer. However, Lee's force did not have it all their own way. *Darwin* was hit be two 5in shells, which started a fire in her ready use lockers on the platform deck. This was a serious fire and *Lookout* went alongside to play water hoses onto the fire.

The enemy cruiser was the last to sink. She rolled slowly to starboard, with her bilge keel exposed, then after a short pause, she sank by the stern. They could here men splashing in the water. "Chief, ask *Meteor* to standby survivors, if they don't want themselves to be rescued, so be it, but don't hang around."

Thirty mins later, *Darwin's* fire was out. *Meteor* had collected ten prisoners. Lee ordered his force to retire towards Ironbottom Sound. Andy Watson moved towards Lee's chair. "Cuppa, sir? Do you know you are the first Royal Navy Captain to sink a German, Italian and Japanese warship? Well done!"

"Thanks, No1, never thought about it, but it's nice to hit back after the pounding we took in the Med. Yes, cuppa would be nice."

For the next few days, the individual cruisers went north, with a couple of destroyers to try to interdict any more enemy ships, but none were spotted. Apart from *Leander*, who found a small coaster trying to sneak south, that was soon dealt with. They also participated in a few bombardments for the Marines to help winkle out the last few pockets of enemy resistance.

Two days later, he watched as *Georgic* entered the sound, her decks packed with aircraft, a fleet of lighters and landing craft, and strange little vehicles called DUKW, or Ducks for short, an amphibious lorry, hurried out to meet her, and start the unloading. "OOW, get my launch ready, I want to go to *Georgic*."

"No 1, do you think Mr Morris can get me over there without getting me wet?"

Watson laughed. "If he does, sir, he will be pushing *Stockport* home." They both laughed.

Onboard *Georgic*, Lee was happy to see Pat again, and over lunch they exchanged stories. Lee informed him about the sinkings — they had lost an Avenger and three Wildcats due to enemy action operating out of Henderson, thankfully only one pilot injured. Admiral Isaacs had asked Alan if *Big G* could make another trip to Bora Bora, and they would replace all the lost aircraft. Apparently, there was a resupply force on its way due in three weeks' time, so once they got here, they would be stood down, and could return to Australia. This suited Alan; some of the destroyers and *Magpie* were having engine problems that needed dockyard assistance. With the Americans Naval Force was a destroyer repair ship, and this had managed, with limited resources to assist with some of the urgent repairs.

Two days later *Big G* sailed again, with three US destroyers as escorts. Force 'Y' still went out on night patrols, but apart from two minesweepers caught and sunk by *Bellona, Meteor,* and *Lively*, the rest was quiet. *Wren* had a bit of excitement when she attacked a submarine contact and claimed a sinking. The Americans didn't give it, they thought it was a shoal of fish but *Wren* was adamant it was a small sub.

Lee was sitting at his desk, reading the messages from his ships. *Blue Rover* was reporting less than 30% furnace fuel oil remaining. Petrol 40%, and 20% Diesel. *Empire Brecon* was down to 40% food stocks. *Lively* and *Lavish* had major problems with their engines and *Magpie* was having boiler trouble. He thought about the miles they had steamed since leaving the UK. His ships engineers had done miracles. Now it was time to go home. Taking Ray Arnold with him, they went across to see Admiral Issacs.

A week later, *Georgic* returned along with a US Navy Tanker and supply ship, the advance party of resupply ships. True to his word, *Blue Rover* was refilled and *Empire Brecon* resupplied, and after *Georgic* had unloaded, the Admiral had insisted the six of the new Hellcat fighters and six brand new Avengers were to be left onboard *Georgic* as a thank you.

Two days later, just as Force 'Y' were ready to sail, a huge fleet of ships entered Ironbottom Sound. The resupply was here! As they headed towards the boom, every American ship cheered ship for the Royal Navy. Best wishes ringing in their ears, and a big thank you from the Admiral. Just before sailing, Lee had paid his respects to Admiral Isaacs and Captain Goodman, taking two more cases of whiskey with him. This went down a treat with both officers. So now they headed home, their aircraft already circling, ready to land on, back at last.

Chapter 11

The pilot of the Avenger never saw his attacker. He was flying far to the east of the fleet and had just commences his turn to the next leg of his search pattern, due south for thirty mins, then head for home. His engine had been playing up, but at the moment it was OK. The Observer had just past him a flask of soup, and a corn beef sandwich. He balanced the flask on the windscreen coaming and started to unwrap his sandwich. He looked up as his flask lifted into the air, how strange, he thought, as it exploded and showered him with hot tomato soup, not that he felt it, as his chest exploded, when the Japanese 20mm shell exited it. The Zero swept down past the stricken aircraft, the pilot looking at the crew of the Avenger. The pilot looked dead, as did the gunner in the turret. The observer was frantically trying to do something behind himself. The second Zero strafed the cockpit area, aiming at the surviving aircrew, and bits of the cockpit disintegrated and fell away in the slipstream. The Avenger slowly turned onto its back and crashed into the sea. If they had stayed on this course, they would have overflown a Japanese naval task force. This was part of operation I-Ho, to retake parts of the Solomon Islands. The Zeros were from the carrier *Katsuragi*, along with *Amagi*. The battleship *Hiei*, plus two heavy, two light cruisers, and seven destroyers. These ships had just entered the Coral Sea and had spotted the Lone Avenger.

Pat Byrne was worried, another Wildcat had aborted take-off, yet again it was water in the fuel — this had been four occasions today. He called his Chief Engineer to go find the problem. He also contacted *Blue Rover*, and asked them to test the petrol, for water. The reply was soon forth coming: there was water in the aviation petrol tanks. And no water in the fuel onboard *Rover*, so the tainted fuel had come from the Americans, when she fuelled at Bora Bora. He contacted Lee over TBS. "Sorry sir, we will have to empty all the tanks off petrol, purge the pipes, also drain all fuel from the aircraft and do the same purge on the tanks and fuel lines."

Lee groaned. "Not your fault, Pat, how long to complete the job?"

"Sir, about six to eight hours, then we will have to refuel from *Rover*, so about twelve to fourteen hours altogether. We can filter some fuel from the aircraft that had not received the contaminated fuel, that should give us about four Wildcats and a couple of Avengers at deck ready, but if we use them there will be nothing left. Also, I am an aircraft missing; he reported a problem with his fuel, but he is an hour overdue, so I guess he is down somewhere."

Lee groaned again. "Damn Pat, what a shocking way to lose men. I suppose we can't send a search aircraft?"

"We could, sir, but we would use what fuel we had, and the destroyers are not in good shape to go looking."

Lee, "OK, Pat, do what you can. Pass me their names and I will send it to the Admiralty as missing. Damn I hate this." He swore badly.

"Captain, Radar Office on the phone."

"Thanks, Pilot." Lee picked up the phone. "Captain."

"Sir, the air search Radar has gone down, a problem with the aerial. We don't have any spares, so it's out till be get back to port."

Again, Lee swore. His magnificent ships were letting him down! "OK Chief, contact the rest of the force, tell them we are blind for now. Messenger, cup of strong tea please." Nobody spotted the dot on the horizon.

The afternoon continued. Lee was sat in his chair, having a few minutes of peace, the sun beat down and there was a certain lethargy around the bridge.

"Captain, message from *Magpie*."

"Go ahead, Bunts." Lee was awake.

"Sir, *Magpie* is saying she has had to shut the boiler down, the furnace bricks have failed."

"Damn, ask them how long for repairs, then ask *Empire Brecon* to take *Magpie* in tow. We can't hang around here." Lee was starting to get worried.

"Reply, sir, from *Magpie*, at least eight hours, and *Brecon* is dropping back to pick up the tow."

"Very good."

As their Nakajima B5N Scout bomber, nickname *Kate* to the Allies, droned on, the pilot was thinking about his evening meal of noodles and salt beef, and a glass of beer. He felt a tug on his left shoulder; his Observer was pointing to the left. He could just make out ships on the horizon. Being an old hand at this, the pilot immediately looked for cloud cover and for any enemy aircraft. He slowly moved from cloud cover to cloud cover, getting ever nearer to the enemy ships. Between the pair of them, they spotted a cruiser, a carrier, and some supply ships, all heading to the southwest. Once he was happy with his report, he made the observer pass it by radio in plain language, back to their Carrier, the *Amagi*. Once the message had been sent, he checked his petrol gauge; there was enough fuel for another twenty mins, then he would have to leave. He moved a little closer to the rear most ships. It looked like the cargo ship was towing the warship, very interesting. "Sumio, pass that back to the carrier as well," he commanded. "OK, time to go back." He turned to the right and headed back to his meal, happy with his work.

The bridge tannoy spoke, "Captain sir, code room here, enemy transmissions close by."

Lee swore, "Bloody hell, where from? Any direction, No. 1, action stations."

The ship awoke from its lethargy. He left the bridge and made his way to the code room.

"Sir, we have picked up a transmission about forty miles away; we are certain it was an aircraft, and while we can't break the cypher, we are pretty certain it is a spotting report about us also sir, the yanks passed us a message, which we have just decoded, stating that a Jap carrier task force is about to enter the Coral Sea from the east. We have no composition of the numbers, sir."

"OK Dave, keep me updated." Lee left for the bridge. Damn a carrier fleet, and his only cover was unusable, due to poor fuel, what to do. He picked up the TBS phone. "*Georgic*, this is father, over."

Pat's voice came over the airwaves. "Go ahead."

Lee quickly explained what he wanted. He ordered all usable fuel to be put into the new Hellcat fighters and any Wildcats, if any left, and have them on flight deck standby. To the rest of his force, he ordered *Bellona* to the east, so just in visual range, to act as a Radar warning outpost. *Brecon* to abandon *Magpie*, take the crew off and sink her, all ships to match *Georgic's* top speed and head SW. He wanted the supply ships and *Georgic* in the middle of his force, with the cruisers and destroyers and *Wren* disposed in a circle around them. He ordered his Communications to transmit to Sydney asking for fighter protection. There was nothing left to do but wait.

"No 1, send the men to dinner, watch by watch, but keep extra lookouts on duty."

Nothing happened. The night came upon them. He regretted having to sink *Magpie*, but at the time it looked like a good idea. An uneasy calm settled across Force 'Y', as they raced SW at twenty knots. Lee went to his sea cabin to try to rest. His steward Bob Pardoe was shaking his arm. "Sir, sorry to wake you. It's thirty mins to sun up, and the ship is at Dawn Action stations, cuppa char for you."

Lee stumbled onto the bridge; he was still fretting about the sinking of *Magpie*. He looked around the bridge, as the sun started to peep above the horizon, faces started to emerge.

The Chief yeoman sang out, "Sir, *Bellona* signalling, large force of aircraft from the northeast."

"Thanks Chief, order *Georgic* to launch aircraft, all ships take independent evading action. Guns, open fire when in range, good luck everybody." He watched as *Bellona*, was hidden by large waterspouts; she emerged spitting fire at the enemy, clearly the Jap flyers were going to take out the radar picket first.

Lt Cdr Akira Watanabe, sat in his Aichi D3A Navy Type 99 Carrier Bomber, known as a Val to the Allies, looked down at the sea judging the swell and wind direction. He had ordered part of his strike force to sink the outlying warship. Twelve Vals, and twelve Kate aircraft set about their task. The warship was twisting and turning, as she sought safety. Watanabe was happy; these were still the cream of the Japanese navy pilots, the remnants of the mighty forces that had ravaged the Pacific for a year. They knew their jobs. He watched with grim satisfaction, as they made a concerted attack with torpedoes and bombs. The warship, staggered and swung to port, black smoke pouring from her funnels and the huge hole torn in her stern section. As he circled, he spotted two torpedoes racing in from port. They slammed into the cruiser.

Bellona staggered and shuddered. Captain Wilkinson knew his ship was doomed. The two torpedoes had wrecked his engine and boiler rooms. She split into two parts, and slowly began to sink, showing a defiant 'V' to the enemy.

From a distance, Lee watched *Bellona's* death throws, "OOW, take a note of the position of *Bellona's* sinking. Get that of the Pilot, and send it to Sydney. They may be able to send a search party out later."

He felt sick. She had been with him from the start. It was like being back in the Med. loosing ships all over again. No time to dwell, the enemy aircraft were approaching. *Stockport's* main battery commenced firing, soon followed by *Leander* and *Darwin*. *Wren* was the rear most ship, and he could just hear the whip crack as she let loose with her four in guns. Ives, *Stockport's* Gunnery Officer, concentrated his main battery on the low flying torpedo bombers and his High Angle guns, along with everybody else, on the dive bombers.

Onboard *Georgic*, Pat watched fascinated. With precision timing, the enemy dive bombers peeled off from a dozen different angles and heights, and in quick succession. They then descended down to deck level to press home their attack with machine gun fire. At the end of ten mins of flaming violence, *Georgic* had been smothered by seven bombs and a near miss on the stern. Like a drunken sailor on a night out, she hauled out of line, flying the 'not under control flags.' The flight deck no longer existed, and half her defensive armament were destroyed. Had she been a "proper" warship, instead of a converted merchant ship, she might have stood a chance.

But not now — she was doomed. All Pat could do was to get as many crewmen as possible to safety.

Wren came along side to assist. As if out of spite, two bombers targeted *Wren* while she was doing her mercy work. She capsized and sank very quickly, taking many survivors from *Georgic* with her. *Georgic* did not sink straight away. She just got lower in the water as if defying her tormentors. This helped the other ships in the force because the prize for the attacking pilots was to sink a carrier, and while she was still afloat the enemy concentrated on her.

Empire Brecon was in a bad way. Hit by a torpedo and two bombs, she was burning fiercely. She lay dead in the water. The fire reached the small arms magazine, and the steady, crackle and bang was heard as the ammunition 'cooked off'. Even with *Magpies* crew onboard, they were losing this battle. *Blue Rover* had a charmed life; her skipper handled her like a destroyer, weaving and dodging. She remained intact, apart from the strafing, which the Japanese aircraft took particular delight in carrying out. The last couple of Val's were passing *Rover*, when the gunners managed to hit one. It staggered under the gunfire, and rose slightly in the air. It was clear the aircraft was doomed. Strangely it turned back towards *Rover*, and dived straight into the bridge structure, which caused a huge explosion. Everyone on the bridge were killed instantly, and *Blue Rover* started to turn to port away from the rest of the ships.

As the enemy droned away, Lee had time to take stock of what had happened. *Bellona*, *Empire Brecon*, *Wren*, and *Georgic* were sinking or sunk. *Blue Rov*er was ablaze. *Lavish* had disappeared; no one saw her passing. *Leander* had a bomb hit on her quarterdeck and could only make fifteen knots. *Lively 's* port engine had failed, so she also could only manage fifteen knots. The aircraft that *Big G* had launched had managed to down three Val's, four Kate's and two Zero's. Now they had nowhere to go, so they circled the fleet until the fuel ran out and then ditched alongside the nearest ship. It was a poor return for the loss of so many fine ships and brave men. Lifesaving operations commenced as many survivors as possible had to be rescued. Lee had no intensions of leaving them here.

When he landed back onboard the fleet flagship *Amagi*, Lt Cdr Akira Watanabe could not understand why a second air strike was not ready to take off. He jumped from his plane and ran to the bridge. The admiral was sat in his chair, drinking a cup of green tea. "Sir, we need another strike to finish of the British ships; they are getting away," Watanabe pleaded.

The Admiral looked up. He was not a carrier man but set in his way's battleship officer. Patronizingly he said, "Ah, Watanabe, there you are, we have orders to proceed to Rabaul, striking at the Americans at Guadalcanal on the way. YOU have lost me fifteen aircraft in that strike against the British. I will not lose any more." With a wave of his hand, he dismissed Watanabe, and went back to his tea.

Watanabe was apoplectic with rage; another strike and that British force would be destroyed. He stormed back to his cabin, mentally writing a letter he would send to his uncle, Head of the Navy Board. If he had anything to do with it, the Admiral would not command a carrier force again.

Lee, of course, did not know any of this. The crews went about their business looking after the dead and wounded, clearing away the spent cartridge cases and bringing up fresh ammunition. Trying to rescue as many survivors as possible. The cooks organised tea and sandwiches to be sent to all the crew members. One good thing, Pat Byrne was rescued, and is now asleep in Lee's Day cabin. He reassembled his force with *Blue Rover* in the middle of a defensive circle. Out of habit, looked over to see what *Georgic* was doing, but she was not there; he felt the pain of her loss. All through the day he kept the crews at defence station, waiting for the Jap planes to come back. By nightfall, it was clear that they would not be returning, so he was able to stand down the men. The adrenalin and shock had now worn off, and the crew started to live with their demons, but the demons did not just come at night. It was a very strong man that said he was not affected. So, they continued on their way to Sydney.

Then three days later, long range Australian Beaufighters appeared overhead; they would stay with them all the way back to port. He received a message saying that a Catalina flying boat had landed and collected eight survivors from *Bellona*, the Captain was amongst them. Apparently, they had been attacked by sharks while in the water, hence so few survivors. Lee retired to his cabin for a few hours and wept for his missing shipmates. He also asked 'The Bish', the ship's spiritual leader, to come and see him.

He received orders that *Leander* and *Blue Rover*, were to proceed to Wellington NZ. *Leander* would be going into the Royal Dockyard for refit, and repairs to the bomb damage. *Blue Rover* was to be taken in hand by a civilian ship repairer. His sadly depleted force was to enter Sydney, where *Darwin* was also long overdue for a major refit at Cockatoo Island. *Meteor* and *Lookout*, after temporary repairs were to proceed to Bombay for refits. *Lively,* however, was found to be beyond economic repair, so would be stripped of any useful parts and scrapped here in Australia. *Stockport* was to proceed to Durban for a major refit. Once docked at Durban, Lee was to be flown home for an enquiry into the loss of so many of His Majesties Ships. Once they were back in Sydney, although very tired, Lee made the effort to visit every one of his ships, to meet the crews and thank them for all their efforts.

Glossary

40mm / Bofors- A Swedish Anti-Aircraft weapon
Adrift — Late/Absent from place of duty
Ashore — Going outside the establishment your living in
Bimble — Walk
Brass Hat,- any officer with gold braid on the peak of his cap.
Bulkhead — Wall
Call the Hands — Means "Get out of bed"
Civvies — Civilian clothing Chum- mate. Chummy ship- ships that work together
Class Leader — A selected member of your class
Clean Ship/Cleaning Stations — Sweeping/Mopping/Scrubbing — Prepare for Rounds
Clubswinger/Clubs — Physical Training Instructor
CPO/Chief Petty Officer — Addressed as "Chief"

Crushers — ships policemen
Daily Dits — Daily Orders
DCT — Director Control Tower, were they aim the guns.
Deck — Floor
Deckhead — Ceiling
Dhobi Dust — Washing Powder
Dhobying — Washing — Usually by hand
Dit — A story or quote usually funny
Divisional Officer — Your "Boss"
Divisions — Formal Parade
Duty Part of the Watch — ratings detailed for additional duties that day
Eytie- slang for an Italian Gash — Baby or new entrant Gizit Freebe or gift.
Goffa — Drink
Guzz — Devonport/Plymouth
H.A.- High Angle weapon used for firing at aircraft.
Heads — Toilets HMS His Majesty's Ship HMIS His Majesty's Indian Ship HMCS His Majesty's Canadian Ship HMAS His Majesty's Australian ship. 'Hooky' Leading Seaman, Leader of a messdeck.
Jabs — Vaccinations etc
Jack Dustys — Supply Chain Logistician

Jap- slang for a Japanese.
Jerry/Nazi/ Kraut slang for a German
Junior Rates — Term for Leading Hands and below
Killick/Leading Hand — Addressed as Leader, Leading Hand or Hooky
Kit Muster — Formal Inspection of your kit
Kye- a thick gluttonous drink made from a block of chocolate and condensed milk.
Make-n-mend — Afternoon off
Matelot (Pronounced MATLOW) — A Sailor/Naval Rating
Maat German Corporal,
Mess/Messdeck — living Quarters
Muster — Collect/gather at a specific location
Nine o'clockers — Later evening meal
No 1/Jimmy — First Lieutenant or Executive Officer
Nozzer — New entrant
Obermaat (Sergeant)
Oerlikon- A Swiss made automatic 20mm anti-aircraft weapon.
Oggin — The Sea/Water
Onboard — Inside the establishment
OOD — Officer of the day
OOW — Officer of the watch
Oppo — Close friend

Parade Drill — Marching and saluting etc
Pipe down — Lights out, go to sleep
Pit — Bed
PO/Petty Officer — Addressed as "PO"
Pom — Pom — 2 pounder anti-aircraft weapon, gets its name from the sound it makes when firing.
Pompey — Portsmouth
Pongo — slang for soldier,
Putty — the shore, ship on the putty, run aground.
Rig of the day — Uniform as specified to be worn
Rounds — Formal Inspection of your messdeck/toilets/bathrooms
Run Ashore — Leisure time down to town
Scran — A Meal
Sea dust — Salt
Secure — Stop work
Senior Rates — Term for Warrant Officers, Chiefs and Petty Officers
Slide — Butter or margarine SNAFU-Situation Normal All F++ked Up.
Snorkers — A Sausage
Stand easy — Short tea break but also a drill order
Stokers/Clankies — The men who attend the ships Boilers

Supper — Early evening meal
TBS, Talk Between Ships, a first generation radio telephone.
Pusser/Pussers — absolutely anything issued by the Royal Navy.
Turn to — Start work
U.S.S. United States Ship.
Vp Boat — German Auxiliary patrol boat, generally a converted Trawler.
WAFU — (Wet and Fucking Useless)
Wet — Any beverage hot or cold
WO/Warrant Officer — Addressed as "Sir"